"What Hurt You So Badly,"

he asked softly, "that you had to run away? Or shall I tell you?"

"No . . . no, I don't want to hear it!" she blurted, her voice thickening with emotion.

Struggling against his superior strength only seemed to excite him, and the low laugh that feathered along her cheek did serious damage to her resistance. She moaned his name, and his answering kiss seemed to go on and on.

"By this time, I know how to handle you, Willy Silverthorne," he murmured. His arms held her captive—not that she would have had the strength to try and escape . . . as he well knew.

DIXIE BROWNING
grew up on Hatteras Island off the coast of North Carolina. She is an accomplished and well-known artist of watercolors but thoroughly enjoys her second career, writing.

Dear Reader:

During the last year, many of you have written to Silhouette telling us what you like best about Silhouette Romances and, more recently, about Silhouette Special Editions. You've also told us what else you'd like to read from Silhouette. With your comments and suggestions in mind, we've developed SILHOUETTE DESIRE.

SILHOUETTE DESIREs will be on sale this June, and each month we'll bring you four new DESIREs written by some of your favorite authors—Stephanie James, Diana Palmer, Rita Clay, Suzanne Stevens and many more.

SILHOUETTE DESIREs may not be for everyone, but they are for those readers who want a more sensual, provocative romance. The heroines are slightly older—women who are actively invloved in their careers and the world around them. If you want to experience all the excitement, passion and joy of falling in love, then SILHOUETTE DESIRE is for you.

I'd appreciate any thoughts you'd like to share with us on new SILHOUETTE DESIRE, and I invite you to write to us at the address below:

Karen Solem
Editor-in-Chief
Silhouette Books
P.O. Box 769
New York, N.Y. 10019

DIXIE BROWNING
Renegade Player

Silhouette Romance

Published by Silhouette Books New York

America's Publisher of Contemporary Romance

SILHOUETTE BOOKS, a Simon & Schuster Division of
GULF & WESTERN CORPORATION
1230 Avenue of the Americas, New York, N.Y. 10020

Copyright © 1982 by Dixie Browning

Distributed by Pocket Books

ISBN: 0-671-57142-7

First Silhouette Books printing April, 1982

10 9 8 7 6 5 4 3 2 1

SILHOUETTE, SILHOUETTE ROMANCE and colophon are
registered trademarks of Simon & Schuster.

America's Publisher of Contemporary Romance

Printed in the U.S.A.

Chapter One

On the last day of May, as on every day since the first week Willy Silverthorne had come to work for Rumark Realty, the low growl of her persimmon-colored 450SL, as it turned off Highway 158 onto Bittern Drive, signaled an exodus from office chairs so that by the time Willy tooled the little sports car into the parking lot behind the office complex familiarly known as the mushroom patch, every window was filled—every window, that is, except one: the last and largest in the Collier Consulting Engineers Building.

As she whipped the polished thoroughbred into the employees lot, passing all the more plebeian vehicles parked in what was already sweltering sunshine, and took her place in one of the only three shaded spots, there came a collective sigh from the three surrounding octagonal buildings.

"Power glide," murmured an agent in the office of MacNulty Insurance. He watched reverently while Willy collected her purse and crossed the softening asphalt to the building that housed Rumark Realty.

"That one's built for speed and handling," sighed a design engineer in CCE.

It was perfectly natural to refer to Willy Silverthorne in automotive terms; her greatest enthusiasms at the present time were cars and food, not necessarily in that order. By the time Willy had worked in the mushroom patch for three days, every man in all three office buildings, whether married or not, had latched on to every bit of information available about her. The few women, if only as a matter of self-defense, were not far behind.

By the time she had finished her first month as a newly licensed real-estate saleswoman, Willy had tactfully refused dates with all but three of the men who had asked her, and had made fast friends with the only other woman at Rumark Realty, Dotty Sealy, a bouncy brunette who worked as general secretary while she studied for her own license as a realtor.

On the morning of June first, it was nine-fourteen when the rush to the windows commenced. Willy was seldom, if ever, on time, a fact that did not seem to bother her boss, who was one of the three men she dated. Today each window held at least one viewer and this time Willy might have sensed a new element of expectancy in the air, had she even been aware of her audience.

As usual, she down-shifted and slowed her 450SL up the slight grade into the lot, then gunned the motor for the final maneuver that would position her in the space marked MR. COLLIER, between Ed MacNulty's Cadillac and the late-model station wagon bearing the logo of her own firm.

The sound of rubber screeching on asphalt could be heard clearly above the drone of the central air-conditioner and it brought several masculine looks of commiseration, plus a few of smug satisfaction—these from the men who had never broken through Willy's friendly but impregnable barrier—and from the office that had stood empty since Randy Collier's leaving; both sets of expressions would have given Willy more than a moment's misgivings had she been able to see them.

There was a car in her place! A superb piece of machinery she recognized as a Porsche, although the exact model was unfamiliar to her . . . as was the owner. Dumbfounded, Willy sat in her car and stared for several minutes before reversing thoughtfully and backing into a place in the sun.

She had used that particular parking spot ever since her second date with Randy Collier. He had volunteered to park his own car somewhere else, claiming the white top was less vulnerable to the heat than was the black top of her dusky-orange Mercedes, and then, after Randy had left Nags Head under conditions she preferred to forget, it had seemed silly to stop parking there. After all, no one had come to take his place as head of CCE, and while his office went unoccupied, she continued to park there with all the aplomb of a girl who had been materially, if not emotionally, spoiled by an indulgent parent for the first nineteen of her twenty-one years.

Her aplomb might have suffered a bit had she been able to see behind the tall, tinted window of the largest office of CCE. The man who stood there observing her leisurely and belated arrival wore no admiring expression. His obsidian eyes were narrowed in a face that was lean to the point of tautness, the muscles of his broad shoulders bunched slightly as he stroked an aggressive jaw thoughtfully with one well-kept hand. The morning sun, rendered impotent by the gray thermal glass, cast shadows under his well-defined cheekbones and the high forehead that was tanned to the color of raw teak. Not a strand of his black hair was out of place, although a lock in the front seemed inclined to rebel, and there was nothing about his summer-weight, custom-tailored business suit to indicate other than a sophisticated man with the wealth to indulge his cultivated tastes.

And yet there was an element about him that was alien to an office setting, that had nothing to do with the dictating of letters or the drafting of company policies. There was a quality of danger about the man, of raw, sensual power that could quell with the lift of a brow and inflame, in the case of a woman, with the same gesture, for few women would be immune to such blatant masculinity.

Certainly not the woman who stood at his side, a slightly smug look of superiority on her flawlessly groomed face. "Well, now you've seen what all the men in the mushroom patch are drooling over. Whatever signals she's sending out with that . . . that come-hither walk of hers remain a mystery to me, I can assure you, but she has every man in all three buildings panting after her and you can't tell me it's all for nothing."

"I suspect the walk you find questionable is merely a natural result of her construction. Wide hips, long legs," Kiel Faulkner murmured absently, not sparing his secretary a glance. Instead, he continued to stare thoughtfully after the tall, slender figure disappearing up the ramp that led to the Rumark Building. There was nothing in particular visible from his present vantage point that would explain the general masculine reaction to the girl whose parking place he had just commandeered, nothing except for a walk that, if she could bottle and sell it, would net her a cool fortune.

"What was it *this* time, a freighter come ashore and you had to call the Coast Guard?" Dotty Sealy gibed with exaggerated patience.

Willy grinned. "Hang gliders. There were three all set to go off the top of Jockey's Ridge and I just had to stop and watch. One of these days I'm going to—"

"No you're not," Dotty finished for her. "Not until they install elevators on Jockey's Ridge, you're not."

Willy's natural laziness was well known. It was not really a disinclination to work, for she did her share and then some, often taking over for one of the other two agents when they had to go out unexpectedly, or staying on without demur to finish up a report that had to go out. She did everything at her own relaxed rate of speed, but that was not to say she didn't accomplish more in the long run than Frank, who came early and stayed late, or Pete, who rushed madly wherever he went. As in the case of the hare and the tortoise, the tortoise in the form of Willy Silverthorne often ambled across the finish line well ahead of the others. As even now she was ambling across the thick sand-colored carpet toward the office marked MATTHEW RUMARK, PRES.

" 'Morning, Matt," she drawled melodiously.

"Seventeen minutes late, Wilhelmina. You're seventeen minutes late and yesterday it was twenty-three. How is it that you can break every rule of office behavior I put on the books and still outsell the others?" he demanded with resignation.

Willy shrugged her shoulders under the yellow T-shirt she wore with her denim skirt. "I dunno . . . just

11

lucky, I guess." The lids that half-hid her dark green eyes seemed weighted down with their burden of luxuriant blond lashes.

Matt Rumark shook his head slowly, not even attempting to hide his admiration of the exquisitely modeled face before him. The fact that that face was covered with a fine layer of freckles that its owner did little or nothing to try to disguise did nothing to mar its loveliness, nor did the heavy weight of sun-streaked blond hair suffer for its casual treatment, being pulled ruthlessly back and tied haphazardly with a cotton handkerchief. Willy Silverthorne's beauty was structural rather than superficial, but her true loveliness stemmed more from a genuine friendliness than from any deliberate charm, a fact that, considering her background, was little less than startling. Somehow, her indolent good humor had a way of disarming female competitors and would-be suitors alike, with few exceptions.

"All right, all right, I know when I'm licked," Matt admitted, shuffling through the litter on his desk and coming up with two new folders. "As boss around here, I owe it to the others to rack you up for getting away with what they wouldn't dare, so consider it done. Now, here are a couple of new listings at Hatteras. Want 'em?"

"Sure," Willy answered slowly, slipping off a sandal to scratch a mosquito bite. "If no one else wants them, I'll take them, but what about Pete? He and Connie are expecting again in September and he could probably use the extra."

Matt shook his head exasperatedly. "Willy, love, did it ever occur to you that a competitive staff means more business for everybody? With every agent out hustling to outsell the others, more gets sold, which means more profit for all of us. Profits . . . remember? The old filthy lucre? It's the name of the game, honey . . . it's what keeps the old capitalistic system ticking over. We make more profit, we expand and hire more people, who in turn make more money, and we all pay our taxes and Uncle Sam is fat and happy, and then we make even more so that we can throw it around a little—that way we spread the joy; in my case, to the purveyors of fishing tackle and bonded whiskey; in yours, to the fancy car dealers and top-drawer restaurants. Then, they in turn grow filthy rich and hire more people and pay more taxes and—"

"Hey, I get the message," Willy laughed.

He shook his head sadly. "I don't think you really do, but in case you're worried, no, Pete doesn't want it. Connie doesn't want him to be that far away when she might have to call him to boil water any minute, and before you drag in Frank, let me remind you of one thing: I'm boss around here, and if I say you sell 'em, you sell 'em!"

Willy laughed, a sound not unlike water rushing over small pebbles, and she stood up. "I sell 'em, Mr. Rumark, sir," she surrendered. She was completely unaware of the eyes that watched her almost wistfully as she crossed to the door, eyes that gazed longingly after her five feet, eight inches of convex and concave curves. Nor did she hear the sigh of pure frustration that followed her out because she was already asking Dotty if she knew who the silver Porsche was.

"The who?" Dotty repeated, sliding her glasses back up on her short nose.

"That's what I wanted to know," Willy explained patiently. "I came barreling into the parking lot this morning and just about creamed it. Somebody parked it in my spot, and if I hadn't stood on my brakes, I'd have ended up in the back seat."

"Search me. Must be somebody at MacNulty's or CCE. My wheels came out of Detroit so long ago they've lost their northern accent, and as far as I know, you're the only one around here who runs anything that even approaches a Porsche."

"Mmmm, I'd like to approach it, right up under the steering wheel," Willy murmured, her husky drawl unconsciously seductive as she put away her purse and opened the folders Matt had handed her.

During the remainder of the week, Willy continued to take her place in the sun without comment, leaving the shade to the Porsche, which she had by now identified as a 928S. It had been nice while it lasted and she had felt no compunction using Randy's place, even after he had gone. After all, it wasn't her fault he had mistaken her good nature for something more and ended up in traction and disgrace. She had made it clear to him from the very first that she wasn't interested in anything serious, but her idea of serious and Randy's had been miles apart. Willy had been perfectly willing to go out to restaurants with him or to cook at her apartment for him, and they had both enjoyed the live plays at the beach and the Lost Colony performance. They had danced and laughed together, and when he had followed her up to her apartment one night after a pretty freewheeling party, she had offered to make coffee for him before he headed home, even though she was more than a little disgusted with him for drinking too much.

He had taken her invitation to coffee for something

more, and before she managed to eject him, he had ruined a perfectly good blouse and bruised her rather badly. She had fought back angrily and he had accused her of teasing, which had angered her still more, for she had never deliberately led him on. With the gloves off, it had all come out in the open: either she give him what he wanted or he took it, it was that simple. After all the money he had spent on her, a dumb little office worker, he intended to collect.

Willy's strength under fire had surprised her, and she had managed to throw him out ignominiously, but then, she had never been so frightened in her life; and when she heard the next day that he had wrecked his car before daylight and been found to have an extremely high alcohol content in his bloodstream, she had shuddered and wondered how she could have been taken in by his bland good looks and pleasant manners.

Randy had not returned to CCE. Willy knew that it had been his father's firm and she suspected he must be in a good bit of hot water with the board of directors or whoever reigned in his absence. She didn't ask, nor did anyone tell her, and she had resumed her social life with an occasional date with Matt, who knew from the first that she was strictly a career woman. There was also Richy, the nineteen-year-old who lived with his mother in the apartment below her own. She had met him during spring break when he brought home two college friends, and because she could see that it mattered so awfully much to him to be seen on good terms with an "older woman" Willy had gone along with him, falling into a comfortable sort of friendship that made no demands on either of them. His mother had laughingly accused Willy of baby-sitting for her and it bothered neither Willy nor Richy. He was a convenient escort, and if she paid her own way—and his as well sometimes—then, what difference did it make? It was undemanding and Willy happened to know that Richy had his eye on a girl at East Carolina University and he even went as far as to ask her advice about how to handle a relationship.

By Saturday she was ready for a break. She had managed a trip to Hatteras to check on the new listings and found them highly desirable. They were both owned by the same Ohio couple who were worried about a gas shortage and had decided to sell them both and look for something closer to home.

Willy opened the salt-streaked window in her one tiny bedroom, having closed it during a brief, hard thunderstorm in the night, and allowed the wind to blow in off the Atlantic. It smelled good—far better, to her way of thinking, than the exclusive atmosphere around her father's Hobe Sound home in Florida. This was her kind of beach and she had grown fond of her inexpensive, haphazardly furnished apartment at the end of Wimble Court, despite the fact that she had grown up in a twenty-seven-room Italian-style villa on three acres of the most expensive turf on the East Coast.

On the beach below, several dogs raced after an irascible gull and Willy laughed aloud at the frustration of the motley pack who stood at the edge of the surf and watched while their tormentor glided safely out over the gentle swells. She hadn't been swimming in over a week, thanks to last week's cold spell; but now, with the almost record-breaking high temperatures, the bottle-green water with its blue-white frosting along the shore was an irresistible temptation. She quickly located her favorite three-year-old bikini and within minutes was loping across the single dune that separated the small, shabby court from the Atlantic.

There was not a soul in sight. The few residents of Wimble Court were old beach-dwellers who had long since forgotten the joys of an impromptu swim, and now even the dogs had found another pastime. After flinching from the first chilly spray, she waded out hip-deep, then dived under a breaker, surfacing on the other side with a laugh of pure exuberant joy. Deliver her from the sterile world of chlorinated, fancifully shaped pools where white jacketed butlers stood by with chrome-plated poles to assist anyone who was gauche enough to encounter difficulties.

After half an hour or so of body-surfing, glorying in the feel of tremendous surges of power moving her forward to scrape her naked stomach on a gravelly beach, she waded ashore. The dogs had returned, and so she raced with them on the hard-packed beach in an unusual burst of energy and then veered off in the direction of her apartment, hopping over the soft, sun-heated crest of the dune to climb her outside staircase. She never bothered to lock her apartment when she was in the area, a reaction, no doubt, of a lifetime of having to accept security measures as a matter of course. Whether at home with her grim-faced "companion" or at school with other girls with essentially the same background, she was never able to forget that she was Wilhelmina January Silverthorne, heiress to Jasper Silverthorne, who happened to own several square miles of various cities both in the States and abroad.

It had been the advent of his third marriage, to a woman half his age, coming hard on the heels of her former fiancé Luke Styrewall's fiasco, that had bought Willy her freedom. Freedom she had grabbed with both hands, leaving behind her almost everything she owned except the little Mercedes 450SL she had fallen heir to when Jasper had divorced his second wife on irrefutable grounds. Willy had taken the car because it had given her her first taste of freedom, which was probably why even now she gloried in the feel of a powerful engine under her command. When she had left home she'd gone directly to her mother's only living relative, a crusty widowed cousin—Fred, who had been only too glad to return to his state of single bliss, after having recently been freed from almost forty years of henpecked bondage. He had been full of advice and had urged her to try for her license in real estate.

Cousin Fred had lived in Edenton, but it had been the outer banks of North Carolina that had drawn Willy. She had grown up near the water, both at Hobe Sound and in the South of France, and it had been a constant source of frustration to her that she was never allowed the freedom to enjoy it. When she had finished her course and passed her exams, Willy had applied for, and been accepted by, a small firm of realtors at Nags Head. Here, she was plain Willy Silverthorne, career woman, with no means of support other than what was afforded her by her fairly good brain and her own determination. She was still learning about herself after so many years of being told what she was to like and dislike, and she discovered that she liked to sleep late. She enjoyed driving and cooking. And she loved searching out new restaurants, trying any food with which she was unfamiliar, then trying to duplicate it in her own small but adequate kitchen.

Now, starved after her swim, she made herself a breakfast of shrimp on whole-wheat bread washed down with a mixture of orange juice and Perrier—hardly orthodox, but nourishing, for all that—and then she climbed into a pair of brief cutoff jeans that had lost all but the two bottom buttons on the fly, leaving her stomach bare to the bikini line. She left on her halter, loosening the neck strings, which were beginning to chafe, and wandered out onto her roofless porch.

Here she had all the sunny privacy she could ever want, plus an almost constant breeze that sometimes faltered at ground level, and she intended to sleep in the sun until lunch, take another dip, cook herself something exotic and then, if she felt like it, sleep until dinnertime. Drowsily, she half-decided to hunt up Richy later and see if he was game to go out to a new Greek restaurant she had seen advertised.

The first awareness that she was not alone came gradually, just a vague, uneasy feeling that the sun-induced redness behind her eyelids had changed from reddish to a dark gray-brown. She felt the cold prickle along her spine that told her someone was staring at her and she was suddenly afraid to open her eyes.

In spite of all she could do, her unnatural rigidity must have revealed her alarm, for he spoke. A deep, chocolate-smooth voice with a hint of grit told her not to be alarmed, and she opened her eyes and gazed up what seemed an inordinate length of extremely masculine body to encounter a dark, speculative gaze. He openly scrutinized her half-naked body, making her burningly aware of her thousand or so freckles.

"I'm your new neighbor," the man informed her in a tone meant to reassure, "come begging." He extended a plastic measuring cup and Willy allowed a small, nervous laugh to escape her. "Sugar?" she asked, feeling some of the tension drain away, to leave her curiously limp.

"Actually, dry sherry, if you have any," he replied apologetically, and at her look of surprise, he elaborated, "I'm trying out a new seafood recipe—scallops and shrimp in a sour-cream, cheddar and sherry mixture—and I discovered I'm fresh out of sherry. My . . . the man who packed for me must have considered all opened bottles perks of the job."

Her interest was thoroughly piqued, and not only because of the recipe. Who would have thought such a strikingly masculine-looking man would be interested in cooking? She led the way to the kitchen, hastily tying her straps as she went. She was only too conscious of the fact that her hair, which she had braided earlier to get it out of the way, showed an untidy tendency to escape its confinement and she tugged surreptitiously at her gaping jeans.

Reaching her topmost cabinet, she shuffled her few bottles until she emerged triumphant, waving a dark bottle with a Spanish label. She handed it over and he studied the label, looking up at her with what she thought was a surprised look of respect.

"I was afraid you wouldn't have anything except créme," he admitted with a crooked smile that revealed one slightly chipped tooth among a lineup of strong, straight white ones. He held up the measuring cup and pulled the cork, inhaling appreciatively.

"Take the whole bottle," she offered generously, still perched on the stool she had knelt on to reach the cabinet. Her face was flushed from her nap in the sun and there was a new crop of freckles emerging, none of which, had she but known it, marred her unorthodox appeal one whit as she coiled herself carelessly into a graceful twist. "I know I can never depend on a recipe for the right amount of seasoning. Only taste will tell." She smiled openly. "What do you do with it?"

"Do with it?" the man repeated with a lift of heavy black brows.

"Bake it? Broil it? Chill it?"

"Oh." He grinned. His face relaxed some of the oddly watchful austerity to give her the first hint of what a devastating effect he might have on an unsuspecting female under certain circumstances. "Actually, you're supposed to bake it in cockleshells, after topping it with crumbs. Do you suppose I might be able to find enough shells on the beach along here or has it been pretty well picked over?"

"Well, we're pretty private this far south—residential, mostly—and since most of the residents have long since collected whatever they needed in the way of baking shells and ashtrays, you could probably find enough. But if you're in a hurry, I have a dozen or so and you're welcome to as many as you need."

"Thanks. That's awfully generous of you. Perhaps in appreciation I could prevail on you to help me sample it . . . unless you lack the nerve to sample a stranger's first attempt at shellfish coquilles."

Willy unfolded her elegant length from the barstool. "Oh, I'm a purple-heart winner when it comes to bravery in the kitchen," she assured him with her slow, half-shy smile.

"Sounds promising. No purple heart, I sincerely hope, but how about a *croix de guerre?*"

"If you're sure you have enough, perhaps I will come

try a bit when it's done. If I like it, may I have the recipe?" she asked.

"Not unless you agree to help me stuff your shells and do a bit of preliminary tasting. Your taste for sherry may not agree with mine. I like it well-laced."

She grinned more freely now. "So do I, up to the point where it stops tasting like sherry and begins to taste like library paste." She located her shells in a bottom drawer and, after selecting half a dozen of the largest, most perfect, followed him from the room.

"Don't you need to lock up?" he asked. "This may take a while."

Willy glanced up at him, shaking her head. "There're only a few of us living here at Wimble and they're all awfully nice people. Besides," she added with a gurgle, "there's nothing to steal, unless someone covets the rest of my cockleshells."

"Not even your purse? You're the first woman I've run into who can go more than twenty-five paces without a full stock of supplies."

"Well, since I don't lock up, I don't need keys, and since I don't smoke, I don't need cigarettes, and since I assume I'm trading my very good sherry for a sample of your equally good cooking, I won't be needing any money, so why bother?"

He shrugged. "Why, indeed?" he agreed, his well-worn deck shoes almost silent as he led the way down her ramshackle stairs.

"Hey," she called after him as she hopped barefoot across the patch of hot concrete that separated the two frame cottages at the end of the street. "Who are you?"

Turning to see her predicament, he grabbed an arm and pulled her, laughing, into the scant noonday shade beside his garage door. "Sorry . . . I forgot to introduce myself. Kiel Faulkner. And you?" He bent to lift the door, revealing a familiar silver-gray Porsche.

Willy stood on one foot, rubbing her calf with the burning sole of her other one as she gazed raptly at the low, superbly engineered piece of machinery. "So you're the Porsche," she breathed reverently. "It's gorgeous."

He leaned against the side and leveled her a gaze that, had she been looking at him, might have puzzled her. "Are you a fan?"

"I could easily become one," she admitted, stroking the flawless finish wistfully.

"Maybe you'd care to give it a road test sometime?"

Her unbelieving eyes flew up to beseech him. "Could I? Really? The only thing I like better than driving a good car is eating a good meal, and it would have to be Cordon Bleu to compare with this."

He looked at her skeptically. "That's a bit hard to believe, Willy."

"What, that I like food and cars?" she asked, genuinely surprised.

"You certainly aren't the first woman to admire a good car, but you're the first I've run across who put them in the same category as food. Come on, this way up." He indicated the stairs in the corner of the garage that comprised the first floor of his cottage.

"Well, I don't see why not," she said, following his long, powerful legs in their trim-fitting chinos. "They're both fun. I get a kick out of feeling all that horsepower under my hands, but when I'm hungry, no mere automobile can compare with hot, thin, lace cornbread, dripping with butter, and fried bluefish that just came out of the surf half an hour before it was popped into the pan. Now, that's my idea of heaven." She followed him into a room that was approximately the same size and proportions as her own living room, but there the resemblance ended.

"I think there's a flaw in your reasoning somewhere along the line, Willy, and besides, that strikes me as pretty mundane fare here on the banks, especially for a gal who appreciates a better line of sports cars."

"Oh, I assure you, when it comes to food, I'm no snob." She settled back into a circular chair of rattan and white leather and watched as he put out a plate of pink shrimp, white scallops, and a bowl of grated cheddar.

"All right, Willy Silverthorne, let's say the magic words and turn this into something that'll melt your heart." He got out the container of sour cream and a large mixing bowl and proceeded to put the ingredients together while Willy looked on in rapt admiration, never once wondering how he came to know her name when she hadn't mentioned it to him.

Chapter Two

That was the beginning of a relationship Willy found increasingly satisfying, although something deep inside her whispered a warning that she must not allow herself to forget the lesson she had learned a year ago in Florida.

On that first Saturday, after sampling the bubbling hot coquilles along with fresh spinach salad and German wine for a late lunch, Willy and Kiel Faulkner spent the rest of the afternoon in his house listening to his favorite Bizet opera, *The Pearlfishers*.

Never one to stand when she could sit, nor to sit when she could recline, Willy found herself relaxing on a down-cushioned sofa under windows that opened to let the salt breeze blow in over her. She had run back to her own place long enough to change the skimpy halter for a T-shirt and she wished now she had taken time to change her shorts as well, as she tugged the shirt down over her gaping jeans. Closing her eyes to the strains of the haunting music, with its counterpoint of raucous gulls and seething surf, she was totally content, and once, when she opened her eyes to see Kiel's gaze on her freckled abdomen, she tugged at her shirt again and apologized for her attire. "Sorry about that." She grinned lazily. "I've gained three pounds since I came here and I haven't gotten around to sewing on all the buttons I've popped off."

Kiel surveyed her frankly, his eyes appreciating her offbeat but very potent style of beauty. "Don't mind me . . . I just live here."

Rolling over on her stomach, Willy cupped her chin in her hand. "It's a great place, isn't it? I've been here several months now and I hope I'll still be here by the time I'm drawing social security."

"Somehow, when the time comes, I doubt that you'll be counting on a social-security check for subsistence," Kiel said, his eyes straying from her heavy crop of sun-streaked hair to the bare feet that waved in loose time with the music. "I expect there'll be a long line of men who'll be delighted to offer you something a good deal more substantial than that. Matter of fact, I've met several of them at the office." His easy smile was not reflected in eyes so dark they seemed to absorb the light, but then, Willy was too well fed and relaxed to notice that fact.

Nevertheless, she wasn't eager to talk about the men at CCE, nor about the one who had left, the one whose place Kiel had taken as head of the firm. "Maybe," she admitted dubiously, "but it's a good feeling, being your own boss. I don't think I'm anywhere near ready to trade that freedom in on a husband, no matter how much security he offered me."

"Who said anything about a husband?" Kiel quipped laconically as the last record came to a clicking end.

Willy slanted him a puzzled look, and then with a dismissing moue she said, "Nobody, I guess. I just assumed—"

"Women often do. Assume, that is," he added enigmatically, unfolding his considerable length to turn off the stereo. The sound quality was superb, but then, Willy was no stranger to first-rate quadraphonic speakers and she merely told him she liked the opera. "It's far more romantic than *Carmen*, isn't it? I think, with a few more hearings, I'll fall in love with it."

"You'll have to come over and listen often then. Feel free anytime."

Feeling a wave of warmth that had nothing to do with her morning in the sun, Willy stammeringly backed out of her gauche remark, but he dismissed her embarrassment with the wave of a hand.

She refused his offer of dinner and afterward wondered why. He hadn't made any threatening moves, nor was there the slightest indication of wolfish tendencies, although he had allowed his eyes to enjoy openly what she supposed she had presented. She wasn't unused to being stared at, though, since she had filled out little more than a year or so ago. Still, there was something about the man that made her wary and she decided that in the case of Kiel Faulkner, she'd better tread carefully. Even the name sounded dangerous, she thought, unconsciously comparing him with Randy Collier. Randy had been one thing . . . she had been able to handle him well enough, as unpleasant as it had been; but she had an idea that if she ever found herself in the same position with this man, she'd come out second-best, and the most frightening thing about the idea was that she wasn't at all sure she'd mind.

Kiel didn't relinquish his parking place in the shade, nor did Willy expect him to. Even when the sun-baked leather burned the backs of her legs so that she was forced to bring along a towel to sit on, she accepted as perfectly natural the fact that Kiel Faulkner took his place with the other heads of firms, leaving the less-desirable places to the working force of the three office buildings. The fact would have dumbfounded her father.

One day during the middle of the week, an exasperated Pete came in with his five-year-old son in tow. Connie, it seemed, was prostrated with a siege of morning sickness and the girl who usually looked after young Kip had failed to show up.

"I don't know how much I can get done with his help," Pete said resignedly, "but it's a cinch I can't leave him home while Connie's out of action. He'd dismantle the place in no time flat. Going to be an engineer, this one."

Somehow, it evolved that Willy ended up spending the morning playing with the child while she listened for the phone. The others, with the exception of Dotty, who had a batch of rush letters to get out, were all showing properties, and Willy made a new discovery about herself: she had a knack for getting along with children. Or at least with one small boy, with a stubborn streak and unflagging energy.

They played cars, using ashtrays and the box that Dotty's staples came in, and Kip was delighted with Willy's ability to vocalize the various engine noises. He was best at horn sounds, himself, and the two of them were thus engaged when Kiel walked in and discovered them on their knees, bottoms up, playing at stock-car racing.

"I wondered just what it was you did over here, Willy, while the real salesmen were out beating the bushes for hot prospects."

She rolled over on the carpet and sat there dusting off her bare knees as she grinned up at him. "Well, the truth will out. I push boxes around under the desk and make noises in the back of my throat. Were you looking for Matt?" Dotty had gone out to lunch early since Willy was there to cover for her.

"No, I came to see if you'd like to go to lunch," Kiel said, stooping to lift the curious boy and sit him on top of Willy's littered desk. "What about it, son, you hungry?"

Kip stared solemnly at the impressive stranger and finally nodded his head silently.

"I had planned to wait until Dotty got back," Willy told him, "but I don't suppose it matters all that much. If anyone calls and we're not here, they'll call back if it's important."

"You must be a valuable addition to the firm," Kiel gibed, extending her a hand.

"Well, to tell the truth, things aren't all that busy around here lately. I haven't had a call all morning, and besides, now that you mention food, I'm starving. So's young Kip here, I'll bet. Pete said he'd be back in time to take him home for lunch and a nap, but something probably came up."

They went to a seafood sandwich place nearby and Willy tried to think what a five-year-old might enjoy, only to have the matter taken out of her hands when Kiel ordered without bothering to consult anyone.

"So," he said over soft-shell crab sandwiches, with milk for Willy and Kip and beer for himself, "as well as being charmingly domestic, you're touchingly maternal. Are you looking forward to settling down and raising a brood of your own as soon as you can find someone to support them all?"

Puzzled by a strange note of mockery underlying his teasing, she nevertheless answered him seriously. "I don't know the first thing about children. Kip is the first one I've ever met at close range, but if he's any example, I'd say I enjoy them. At least we seem to have a few interests in common."

Kiel laughed at this, and Willy watched, fascinated at the play of muscles under the tanned skin at the throat of his open-necked shirt. The tension eased and she thought she must have imagined the sarcasm. They finished off with coffee for the adults and a small ice cream for Kip, and Kiel wondered aloud if Willy had to forgo all desserts in order not to pop any more buttons off her jeans.

"Certainly not," she admitted ruefully. "I don't have all that much self-discipline. I was a bean pole up until a year or so ago, when I finally started filling out a little." She ignored his look of patent disbelief. "Something to do with my metabolism, I guess. I can eat voraciously and all it does is make me sleepy."

"I'd have said your metabolism was set at slow idle, but then, maybe I only see you at your gluttonous worst. You probably starve yourself between dinner dates," he teased.

Whatever answer she might have made was forestalled when Kip climbed drowsily into her lap, managing to smear chocolate on her blouse and spill her purse on the floor. She smiled indulgently at the child and allowed Kiel to gather up her belongings, and then he took the boy from her and carried him out to the car, where he settled him on her lap again for the short drive back to the office.

Pete turned into the parking lot behind them and Willy introduced the two men, handing over the querulous child to his father.

"Call me again when you get hungry," Kiel gibed, leaving her on the divided ramp that led to the two offices, and she went inside to hear the strident summons of the telephone, which more than made up for its morning silence during the rest of the afternoon.

Willy sold a forty-seven-year-old house at Coinjock that had been on her list of the ten least likely to sell and was given a new condominium, as well as a dilapidated rental house that was threatened by every high tide. She took what came her way, did her easygoing best, which usually happened to be as good as, if not better than, that of the other two agents and Matt; and when her commissions added up to her monthly rental plus a reasonable amount left over for running expenses, she was satisfied. She had found out early in life that money brought with it its own attendant problems, and as long as she had enough to eat and a place to sleep, she'd be perfectly happy. As for clothes, she had enough to last her for the time being, especially since she lived in casual skirts and jeans, plus the occasional long cotton gown for more festive evenings; when winter rolled around, she'd get the rest of her things out of storage and try not to be embarrassed by her father's ostentatious idea of suitable winter coats for a young woman.

Saturday was drizzly and sleepy, the sort of soft, gray weather she loved along the beach strand. She slept late and then spent several hours rereading her favorite nineteenth-century ghost stories, and she was about to doze off again when Kiel appeared at her door with his measuring cup and a beguiling light in his dark eyes. She had tried to determine if those eyes were actually black or just a very dark shade of brown and had finally

31

concluded that they were a metallic shade of gray, allowing a viewer no insight at all into the mind of the man behind them.

"What are you begging this time?" She laughed, laying aside her book.

"Any wheat germ?"

"You're kidding!" she exclaimed, getting to her feet in one easy, fluid motion.

"Scout's honor. Read a healthy junk-food recipe calling for honey, peanut butter, wheat germ and stale whole-wheat bread, and I thought this looked like a perfect day to try it."

They collaborated on that one for the next few hours and laughed together when it turned out to be messier than either of them would have believed possible. Kiel sat on one of his cane-topped barstools, thighs spread and elbows propped on the counter as he watched Willy deal with the stack of messy utensils; and it was then, when she stood there helplessly, her hand sticky with honey, that the tenor of the afternoon changed from an easygoing compatibility of two people with mutual interests to something infinitely more interesting and far more dangerous.

Kiel took her wrist, laughing at her with those strangely mocking eyes, and pulled her close to him so that she stood between his thighs, and then he lifted her hand to his mouth and touched her sticky finger with his tongue. While a feeling unlike anything she had ever experienced before crept up her limbs, draining them of all strength, Willy stood there, her eyes hopelessly entangled with his, and allowed Kiel to lick the sweet mess from each finger; and when he slipped her little finger into his mouth and sucked gently, she couldn't hold back a gasp. Just before her knees buckled, he drew her up against his chest, holding her shuddering body tightly between his thighs, and they continued to stare into each other's eyes as his face slowly lowered to her own.

Willy had been kissed before. After a slow, miserable start, due to being an awkwardly tall, skinny, freckled child until her eighteenth year, she had begun to blossom and had learned to her amazement that her own brand of beauty, far removed though it was from conventional prettiness, seemed to attract more than a few men. Of course, by that time, her father had introduced her to Luke Styrewall, and so she had very little opportunity to try her newly metamorphosed wings.

Once she had left all that behind, though, she had quickly learned to refuse without offending in all but the most determined cases, keeping her would-be lovers as friends as often as not. She had enjoyed a few lighthearted flirtations, and when they threatened to get out of hand, she had dealt with them skillfully, with no lasting harm done on either side, except perhaps in the case of Randy Collier; but nothing had prepared her for this . . . this mind-shattering, bone-melting assault on her senses by the man who was tantalizing her mouth with a sensuous barrage that made her want to tear off her clothes, or his, or both, and be done with it!

With the little strength left to her, she backed away, acutely aware of the warmth of his hands as they slipped over her rib cage and lingered teasingly on the soft sides of her breasts. "Whoa," she said shakily. "I think, if it's all the same to you, I'd better stick to soap and water from now on." She held up her unsteady hands, the long, slender fingers bare of any adornment. There was an unfamiliar throbbing at the pit of her stomach that distracted her, and so she missed entirely the curious guardedness that slipped down over his opaque eyes.

"Just as well," he told her easily. "I think the first batch of these things is about ready." He turned casually to the oven, just as if he hadn't melted her down to a puddle of quivering nerve endings with one kiss only seconds ago.

Lord, the man was a positive menace! Was this the way they had felt, all those overamorous men she had dated and danced with and then turned away with a quick good-night kiss? They had looked at her as if she were edible, a slightly sick longing in their eyes that had always made her vaguely uncomfortable, but if *this* was what she had inadvertently done to them, then it was a wonder they even spoke to her afterward!

"Here, try one, but watch out! They're hot!" Kiel placed the pan of brown, crispy-looking bars on a wooden block on the counter and poked gingerly at the one on the end.

That night he insisted on taking her out to dinner. She had declined his invitations before, for reasons she little understood herself. Twice she had told him it was because she had to go to Hatteras and wasn't sure when she'd be back, but perhaps it had been some deepseated protective mechanism she didn't even know she possessed that had begun exerting itself in the face of his threatening attraction.

"There's a new restaurant that does something Mediterranean with seafood. Have you tried it yet?" he tempted her. "I thought we'd dine about nine, and then, by the time we're through, there'll be little enough traffic so that you can see what you think about the handling and road-hugging ability of the Porsche. Aerodynamically, it's much superior to the nine-twenty-four," he assured her, thus setting the hook and reeling her in.

Willy was ready for him by eight-thirty, as he could no doubt tell if he cared to look across the court. She seldom bothered to lower the shades, leaving the lights out, instead, during any critical stages. She had chosen to wear a midi-length dress of cotton piqué in a splashy print of navy, orange and white. It was cool and comfortable and, to an untutored eye, could have cost a fraction of what she had actually paid for it back in Florida. Her hair was piled on top of her head and she slipped on a pair of inexpensive earrings of white enamel as her only bit of jewelry. A splash of orangy red lip gloss, a whiff of light cologne, and she was ready except for her sandals, and she wriggled her feet into those as she surveyed her image in the mirror, approving of what she saw in a perfectly impersonal way. No amount of makeup could disguise the fact of her freckles and so she seldom bothered with using any, leaving her sandy-colored lashes and brows natural as well, instead of having to bother with removing mascara when she came home tired and sleepy.

Willy believed in conserving energy. She didn't mind going to any amount of trouble if she thought a thing worthwhile, but gilding the lily of her personal image meant little to her and she spent as little time and effort on it as she could get by with. She extended a foot and checked the strap of her cork and macrame sandal. It added two inches to her already considerable height, but Kiel could give her several inches, even so. She hadn't realized at first just how tall he was, because of his broad shoulders and the beautifully coordinated way he moved . . . especially in trunks when he had just come from a long run down the beach.

Several times she happened to be outside when he returned from an early-morning jog or a swim, and he had invited her to join him, but she had begged off, preferring to spend her spare time doing something less strenuous.

"All that energy wasted," she had chided on seeing him return from what must have been a three-mile run, considereing the time elapsed since he had crossed the dune. "You might at least be charging a battery or something useful."

"Could be I'm *dis*charging a battery, or at least a buildup of potential energy," he had retorted with a twisted grin. He had allowed his eyes to roam significantly over her bikini top as she leaned over her railing. "There's more than one reason why schools stress sports, Willy girl."

She had not misunderstood him. It had served only to reinforce her own opinion that it wasn't safe to accompany him on his solitary jaunts down the empty beach before daybreak, or to join him in his quick evening swims, either. She had found it virtually impossible to ignore the buildup of a strange sort of tension in herself and considered it wiser not to risk striking any sparks.

Until tonight, that was. Staring helplessly up into the darkly handsome face as she opened the door to him some fifteen minutes later, Willy had cause to wonder if her brain had taken a holiday. This man was no Richy, to be indulged, teased gently and then sent on his way. Nor was he a Randy Collier, either, for that matter, to be flirted with mildly across the safe distance of a restaurant table, danced with under the stars and then turned away with a lukewarm kiss. It had blown up in her face on that dreadful last occasion and it was up to her to see that such a thing didn't ever happen again.

Correction, she told herself: it was up to her to see that she didn't change her mind about what she wanted. No involvement with any man, not since the fiasco engineered by her own father, was going to trap her again. She had escaped that one time by the skin of her teeth and she wasn't going to allow herself to be vulnerable ever again.

"You look ravishing, as I'm certain you know," Kiel told her, his deep velvet voice registering on her whole body instead of only on her ears.

She murmured her thanks, gathered up a cobwebby stole and latched the door behind her. "You'll notice that I *do* take the normal precautions when I'm going to be out," she pointed out, "so you see, I'm not a total fool."

"It never once occured to me that you were," he told her solemnly, handing her into the well-sprung car.

Disdaining the menu, Kiel ordered for them both, an arrogant habit she had noticed without too much surprise before. He selected a dry white port to go with the antipasto, a Rhine to accompany the oysters on the half-shell, and then he ordered both *gamberi alla siciliana*, a succulent shrimp dish, and *scombro ripieno*, skillfully seasoned mackerel stuffed with Romano and mushrooms, which they proceeded to divide and wash down with a well-chilled Riesling.

"Oh, you're killing me with kindness," Willy groaned, reaching over to pick the last mushroom from his plate.

"I never met a more willing victim, then," he came

back, smiling at her in a way that filtered through to the very soles of her feet. "Dessert? No, on second thought, I'll see to that, myself . . . later."

"Forget it," Willy implored. "I couldn't eat another bite!"

They stood up and moved out onto a screened porch where several couples moved lethargically to recorded Italian love songs, and when Kiel took her in his arms, Willy wrapped both her own arms around his shoulders and more or less draped herself on him.

"Kiel, I'm utterly disgusting, I know, but I don't think I can even stand, much less dance. The wine . . ."

"Then just don't put up any resistance and I'll see if a little passive exercise will help matters any." He laughed, swaying her gently from side to side.

She followed him perfectly, for he moved with an easy, natural grace that required little effort on her part, and when she became aware of a certain tension after a while in the way he was holding her, she straightened away from him, allowing her arms to assume a more conventional position.

"Don't change," he murmured against her hair.

"You plied me with liquor," she accused, laughter burbling in her husky drawl, "and what's worse, at least where I'm concerned, you plied me with food that was totally irresistible." She let her head rest against his neck, her eyes on a level with the pulse that beat just under his jaw. She felt satiated with food and drink and something else she didn't dare analyze, something she had no desire to resist.

"Hedonist. You're an amazingly easy target, you know."

She responded lazily to the teasing note in his voice.

"I am, aren't I? I'm making all sorts of alarming discoveries about Miss Willy Silverthorne these days."

His feet slowed to a stop and his arms tightened until she was acutely aware of every muscle in the length of his body. "I think we'd better get out of here or I'm going to start on my dessert beforetimes," he growled, leading her out the screened door and around to where they had left the car. "I'll give you a rain check on that road test. I don't think you're in any condition to appreciate the subtleties of engineering tonight, hmmm?"

They went straight home and Willy suppressed a minor surge of disappointment as he wheeled into his garage. It was too early for the evening to end, especially as she was feeling— How *was* she feeling? Full, but not uncomfortable . . . woozy, but not drunk . . . satisfied, yet strangely unsatisfied. And when Kiel led her across the uneven pavement to the dunes that led onto the beach, she followed along as if she had had a last-minute reprieve.

"Leave your shoes here," he ordered, slipping off his own and turning the cuffs of his white trousers up a couple of turns. He took off his natural linen jacket, turned back the sleeves of his brown silk shirt, and they began to walk.

There was no one on the beach. Between the crests of the high row of dunes, the lights of an occasional cottage glimmered, but for all Willy cared, they could have been alone in the world, so still was the night, so bright the moon; and when Kiel began to speak after they had walked for perhaps a quarter of a mile, Willy had trouble shifting from a purely sensual creature to a rational one in order to grasp his words.

"Why don't you ride to work with me from now on?"

"What? Oh . . ." She considered the idea and rejected it, and Kiel wanted to know why not.

Her refusal had been instinctive, based on the crazy, exhilarating feeling of skating on thin ice she had when she was with him, but she tried to rationalize it. "Oh . . . I don't know, Kiel. It's enough of a coincidence, our working so close and living so close. I mean, who would have expected you accidentally to move into the house closest to mine when we happen to work in adjoining buildings. If we suddenly started showing up for work together, people might— Oh, you know what I mean! So far, no one's even seen us out together, but if we suddenly start letting it be known that we practically live in each other's pockets, then tongues will start wagging and I can do without that sort of thing."

"So you prefer not to mix business and pleasure, hmm?"

Sidestepping a wave that was more aggressive than its brothers, she jostled against him and he caught her to his side and forgot to release her. "I hadn't exactly thought of it that way," she parried.

"Then think about it. Surely you haven't managed to get off scot-free, working with all those would-be Lotharios. Haven't you even dated a few of them?"

She moved her shoulders in a disparaging way, searching for a way to change the subject, but he persisted and finally she told him that yes, she had gone out with one or two of them and still dated her boss on occasion. "But I'd rather not, really," she finished weakly.

"Then why do it?"

"Oh, I dunno . . . line of least resistance, I suppose," she admitted.

His eyes pierced the lambent moonlight to explore her profile. "You're a strange person, Willy Silverthorne," he said finally, halting to turn her in the opposite direction. "Hasn't any man ever got beneath your decorative armor to see what sort of heart beats under all those freckles?"

She shook her head negatively. "No man's tried very hard." She laughed unconvincingly. "I didn't think men were particularly interested in hearts, as such, these days."

"Cynic," he murmured, but his tone was gentle and he urged her into an easy jog, telling her when she protested that unless she ran off about five hundred calories, she couldn't have any dessert.

She loped along beside him, keeping up with him easily in spite of his peak condition, for her long, free-swinging limbs were the equal of his more muscular ones; and when he caught at her arm and swung her around to confront him at the edge of the surf opposite their own street, she was scarcely breathing hard.

"And they told me you were bone-lazy," he teased. "You're like a kitten who sleeps all day long and still manages to outperform any other animal."

And you're like a tiger who sleeps in the sun all day . . . and moves in for the kill when you least expect it, she said silently. Aloud, she asked, "Who told you?"

A cloud passed in front of the moon, obscuring his expression for a moment. "Oh, you've quite a reputation around the mushroom patch, didn't you know?" He was joking. Or, at least, she hoped he was joking.

"That doesn't sound too promising," she said doubtfully.

"It sounded awfully promising to me. Let's see . . . moves like a gazelle, or walks as if she's treading

41

eggshells barefoot, depending on who's doing the talking; always a friendly word for everybody, or nobody gets to first base in spite of all her come-hithering, again depending on who's doing the talking. Shall I continue?"

"I don't think I want to hear any more," she said uncomfortably.

"Why not? I did. I admit freely to being avid, once I heard about this paragon of pulchritude who had every man in three office buildings falling over their own feet for a glimpse of her wondrous attributes. I thought I'd better check it out, see what I'd been missing."

Suppressing an odd shaft of pain, Willy moved away from his side and headed for the saddle-backed dune that gave onto Wimble Court. "And were you satisfied or disappointed?" she asked in a small, tight voice without looking to see if he were behind her.

He caught at her hand and laced his fingers through her own. "Neither," he told her deeply. "Neither, Willy . . . yet. Now, come on. I promised you dessert."

"I think I've had enough to last me a week. I'll pass it up if you don't mind," she told him in a flat tone, swooping down to collect her shoes, her stole and her bag.

He held her hand firmly while he collected his own things, and then, instead of walking her to her door, he paused outside his garage and opened it, passing his car to lead her over to the stairs in the corner. "We'll sample it, nevertheless," he told her, and she hadn't the heart to argue. She could find no excuse for her own weakness and so she ruthlessly smothered the small warning voice inside her.

On the counter, a board of cheeses sat softening, and

after tossing aside his jacket, Kiel took down a bottle of a heavy, sweet Greek wine and handed down two glasses while Willy stared helplessly at the hard muscles of his arms and shoulders, brought into play by the simple action.

"Open the porch door. We'll have it outside if the dew isn't too heavy on the furniture," he suggested, pouring a generous portion into the two glasses and laying a knife on the cheese board. He followed her out, and when she would have taken a chair, he swung her over to the broad redwood lounge with its slightly damp but heavenly soft cushion. She felt the coolness bite into her feverishly hot skin.

Lowering himself beside her where he could easily reach the table, Kiel shaved off a wafer of cheese and dipped it into the sweet wine. "Open wide," he ordered, "and say, ahhhh."

"Before or afterward . . . the ahhh, I mean," Willy gurgled. The combination was irresistible and Kiel proceeded to feed her as if she were a baby, interspersing nibbles of cheese with sips of the ambrosial wine, and he ate from her slices and drank from her glass, turning it so that his lips touched the place where hers had touched.

Once more their eyes caught and held, and when she lost the will to break away, feeling deliciously drowsy from the combination of too much wine, rich food, and the soporific salt air, Kiel placed the glass and the cheese down on the table beside them and drew her unresisting body forward until she collapsed on his hard chest.

He kissed her slowly, as if savoring the richness of the wine, and by some sleight of hand that was beyond her capacity to understand, she found herself lying on top of him, her face tucked into the curve of his neck, and she inhaled the herb-scented soap and slightly musky maleness, a smile quivering on her lips. She daringly opened her mouth and tasted the tautness of his skin and felt his immediate reaction beneath her.

"God . . . Willy, you're ruining me!" he groaned, and his hands did something at her back and she felt the chill of dew on her flesh as the sides of her dress came unzipped.

Fire raced through her body, rousing her from her dreamy state, and she protested. "Kiel . . . no, please."

He didn't reply. Instead, his hands moved over the satiny skin of her back and then slipped under her own weight to cup her bare breasts, and she could feel the swollen softness tightening into hard nubs that pushed against his palms in an involuntary invitation that left her stunned and breathless.

He turned his face and she was drawn inexorably into the vortex of a kiss that rendered her open and vulnerable, a kiss that sent wild emergency signals racing to all the most secret areas of her body; and when she felt his hand smoothing her hips, sliding slowly on the bit of nylon that covered her under the fallen sides of her dress, she panicked. His hand was pressing her even closer to his own muscular body and she began to struggle.

"No . . . please, Kiel," she pleaded, scrambling up to sit trembling on the edge of the chaise. She tugged at her dress, shrugging the straps back up on her suddenly chilled shoulders, but any fastening up was totally beyond her in her present state and she looked around helplessly for her shoes. "I have to go now," she whispered.

"Spoken like a nice, polite little girl. The party's over now and I have to go home," Kiel said bitterly. The moonlight shone down on his dark face, revealing half-closed eyes that seemed to be staring out over her head, and the lines that slashed down his lean cheeks were deeper than ever. Never had moonlight seemed so harsh.

She stood there beside the chaise uncertainly, her stole hanging over one shoulder and her sandals dangling from her hand, and she eyed him cautiously, fascinated in spite of herself. In the stillness of the night, she could hear his breathing and it was far harsher, more ragged than any of the times she had met him when he came from a run along the beach.

"Well? What are you waiting for, absolution?" he ground out at her. Then, tiredly, "Go on home, Willy. You're safe."

Chapter Three

Her own breath was coming in deep, starved gasps by the time she let herself into her dark apartment. Without turning on the light, she allowed her dress to fall to the floor, and within a few minutes, she was courting sleep, willing it to chase away the confusing emotions that had aroused her from what she now knew was an artificial apathy that had lasted almost a year.

For the first time since she discovered that Luke Styrewall, with whom she had thought herself so deeply in love, had been hired by her father to court her, win her and marry her, Willy felt the protective barrier she had erected around her heart begin to crack and fall away. Her instincts warned her that if she fell in love with a man like Kiel Faulkner she'd be taking her life in her own hands. Kiel had none of Luke's smooth, well-modulated charm, being a different breed of man altogether.

Luke's attentions had started soon after she had come home from school in Switzerland. She had been tall, scrawny and unsure of herself in spite of the efforts on the part of her teachers to turn out a finished product. Perhaps the fact that her father had insisted that she call him by his first name had something to do with it, because it was impossible not to notice the way he seemed figuratively to try to sweep her under the carpet whenever he was entertaining any of his glamorous young friends. And the friends seemed to grow younger all the time, to Willy's embarrassment, until she felt as if she had wandered into a reunion of her own classmates.

Luke had come on the scene so smoothly that at first she had paid him no attention, knowing that he would ignore her as did all the other men at her father's endless social gatherings. But this time it was different; this time, the best-looking man in the house had eyes only for Willy, and in the months it took to convince her that he really cared for her, that he saw beauty in her graceful young innocence—"coltish charm" was a phrase he used more than once—Willy fell in love.

There was no pressure on her, nothing to indicate that Luke couldn't restrain his manly impulses, and she thought he was wonderfully forbearing to be so patient. Her own curiosity to sample the delights she had only read about and heard about grew, and when Luke asked her to marry him, she thought she had reached the pinnacle of human happiness. That was the beginning of her blossoming, as if all she had waited for all along was the warmth of his approval and the nourishment of his temperate lovemaking.

Jasper was planning to take his third wife by then, a divorcée named Breda Coyner, who was only half a dozen or so years older than Willy herself. There had been an instinctive animosity between the two women that built tensions in Jasper's Hobe Sound villa, where Breda was a more or less permanent guest even before the wedding.

It came to a question of whose wedding would take place first, Breda's and Jasper's or hers and Luke's, and since Luke was beginning to show signs of wanting more than the tepid engagement, Willy rather thought she might be the first to walk down the aisle. But then she overheard a conversation that was not meant for her ears.

She had taken off her engagement ring to practice the violin earlier in the day, because the slightly ostentatious diamond kept slipping on her finger and distracting her, and she remembered it as she was ready to go to bed. She didn't bother with slippers or a robe, thinking there was no one downstairs at that time of night, but she was wrong; her father and Luke were in the study and the door was partly open so that when she heard her own name mentioned as she passed, it was only natural that she slowed her steps.

"Why don't we say sometime within the month, Luke, and a settlement of, say . . . fifty thousand on your wedding day?"

"Make it seventy-five, Jas. Willy's not the only heiress on the market, you know, and there's—"

"Luke," her father had interrupted impatiently, "I've paid you enough to found an empire already! You've got an assured income for as long as the marriage lasts, so don't try to . . ."

Willy had not stayed around to hear more. The flight of stairs that swept around one end of the foyer seemed as vast and unscalable as the highest mountain, but at last she made it to the doubtful security of her own room. She had curled up into a tight ball, dry-eyed and numb, and allowed the waves of misery and humiliation to wash over her until, sometime before daylight, she had mercifully lost consciousness.

That was on a Wednesday. By the following Wednesday, she was in Edenton, North Carolina, a lovely, historic little town on the Chowan River, gradually thawing out under the gruff, almost impersonal kindness of her mother's cousin, Fred Harbinger. The showdown at her father's home had been hard, fast and furious, and Willy had discovered a side to her personality that had surprised her: she was not afraid of her father anymore. She had his backbone and stubbornness along with her mother's easygoing nature, and she simply told her father that she was leaving and that he could make whatever restitution to Luke he thought fair, considering the broken contract between them. When Jasper had tried to talk her out of it, minimizing the financial settlement, and then had tried to explain that it had all been for her own good, to protect her from fortune-hunters, she had stared at him stonily, still more than a little bit numb, and let him finish.

"I'm twenty, Jasper. I'm going to take enough money from my account to pay for training and then I'm going to support myself, and whether or not we continue to have any relationship at all is strictly up to you. Try to hold me here and I'll hate you. As it is, I only despise you; but let me go and promise not to try to interfere with my life from now on, and you'll be free to start your own marriage to Breda without a troublemaking daughter on your doorstep. And I'll make trouble, I promise you. You have everything to lose; I have nothing at all."

The delivery had been made in a flat, unemotional tone, for she had no emotions left after a night of wakefulness and a day of weeping, and it had been all the more effective for that. Her father had insisted she take the car she had been using, and because it was practical, she had agreed. It had been on the long drive up the coast that she had come to enjoy the feel of an aggressive engine that responded to her every mood, and by the time she had reached Edenton, she had all but erased Luke and Jasper and the house that had never been a home since the day her father had bought it when he married his second wife.

How could she have fooled herself into thinking she was so secure? Willy Silverthorne, self-sufficient career girl who had made a vow that neither man nor money was ever going to throw her into a tailspin again. She'd manage her own life and play whatever games she chose to play according to her own set of rules.

That she had been successful so far was a measure of her own unexpectedly level head. It had come as a total surprise to find that she was not the undesirable creature she had supposed. Men were interested in her—some of them more than interested—without even suspecting that her father could buy and sell half the small towns in any given state, and she had had to come from behind almost every other girl her age in learning how to deal with the fact of her own attractions. That she had been fortunate so far was due partly to her genuine friendliness, partly to a natural indolence that kept her from becoming involved in too many social activities, and partly, she supposed, to pure luck.

And now, just when she was getting along so well, she had to run up against something—some*one*—she was ill-equipped to handle. Vague disquiet followed her into her sleep, making uneasy dreams plague the few remaining hours of night. When the first fingers of dawn stretched up through the low-lying cloud bank out over the Atlantic, she was no closer to a solution than before.

A moderate drinker at best, Willy regretted the wine

she had consumed last night. Each one had been carefully selected for the course and drunk sparingly; nevertheless, it still added up to too much. She tried to convince herself that the wine was responsible for her abandonment last night, but she knew it was not so; she was terribly afraid that in the clear light of day, with nothing more intoxicating than water, she would still find herself shatteringly vulnerable to Kiel Faulkner, and the worst of it was, she *liked* the man so much! It would be easier to deal with physical attraction if it didn't mean losing a friend and playmate she was only now coming to appreciate.

She sat up in bed, staring absently at the moisture beaded on the window screen, and felt the morning coolness pour over her bare body. Above the narrow strip of gray that traced the horizon, the sky was a sultry, colorless bowl, promising another scorcher, and she swung her feet to the floor, knowing exactly what she needed.

Taking time only to brush her teeth, she tugged on her old bikini and dropped down the stairs, two at a time. She made a mental note, which she promptly forgot, to buy herself a new one-piece bathing suit before the season ended, because this one, her most comfortable one of all, was faded colorless and out of style . . . as well as too revealing by half!

The tide was out, exposing a wide expanse of hard sand with a shallow pool and a bar between her and swimmable water. Willy ran, splashing through the shallows, her hair streaming out behind her, and when the water surged around her hips, she fell flat on her face, arms extended, and allowed herself to drift over the sluggish swells.

Twenty minutes later, feeling vastly refreshed, she turned shoreward. Her problems weren't all *that* insoluble. All she had to do was say no when—and *if*—Kiel Faulkner asked her out again. Nothing to it. Why had she allowed herself to get into such a tizzy last night? Now in the bright light of morning, she wondered as much, and it took only the cool, gritty baritone to tell her how shallow had been her spurious security.

"'Morning, Willy." He was seated atop the dune, wearing a pair of navy-blue trunks that weren't much larger than her own bathing outfit, and as he unfolded his lean, hard-muscled length and strolled to meet her, she groaned inwardly and surrendered out of hand. "There'll be ridable swells within fifteen minutes or so, so why don't we wait for one good ride and then go back and have omelets with sour cream, tomatoes, and sweet onions, along with tiny smoked sausages?"

"Oh, Lordy, not again," she protested, only half-jokingly.

The grooves that ran from his proud nose to his chiseled mouth deepened as he teased her with a sidelong look. "I always suit the bait to the quarry. With most women, it's diamonds; with some, a villa in the South of France might turn the trick; but now and then you run up against one of those rare creatures who prefer horsepower and *haute cuisine*."

There was no point in being coy. *She* knew she wanted to be with him and, what's more, *he* knew it too. At least over sausages, omelets and coffee, she wasn't as apt to be seduced, especially as both of them had to be at work in little over an hour. Kiel didn't strike her as a man who would care to be hurried, no matter what course he was intent upon, so she was reasonably certain he wouldn't try to fit more than a swim and breakfast into the time alloted. That meant she was safe.

Or so she rationalized.

Breakfast became a morning habit and so did the morning swim, with Kiel's behavior above reproach, Willy acknowledged with some degree of frustration. And still, it was marvelous fun.

"If I'm not careful," she said one Friday morning as they waded ashore, cool and invigorated after a half an hour of body-surfing, "I'm going to turn into a jock and then there goes my image as a lazybones."

"No chance! You might just turn into the Goodyear blimp, but that's about the extent of it. Tell me something, have you always eaten this much?"

"It's not so *much,*" she argued with mock indignation. "It's just so discriminatingly."

"Yeah, about as discriminating as a garbage truck." He pinched her well-rounded but still-lean bottom, and she swatted his hand away.

"I was a bean pole! I kept on trying to fill up all those places that other girls filled up when they were about fourteen. By the time I found out that I wasn't really patterned after an ironing board, it had got to be a habit."

Looping the towel around her neck, Kiel drew her closer and began rubbing her hair as they stood on top of the saddle-backed dune bathed in a wash of gold sunlight. "What were you like as a little girl, Willy? Somehow, I can't picture you as anything except the disgustingly lazy, ridiculously sexy woman with the offbeat sense of fun."

The last thing she wanted to do was talk about her childhood. Now that the wounds had healed over, she realized that it had not been all that unpleasant . . . only uneventful. Extremely circumscribed by a parent who, after his first wife died, had neither time nor patience to indulge a child, and so had arranged for her to be brought up in a way that didn't disturb the sybaritic tenor of his own life-style.

She snatched back her towel and flicked it at his lightly furred thigh. "Where's that breakfast you promised me? Your turn to cook today," she taunted, loping off toward her own apartment to get dressed.

"Ten minutes," he warned. "One minute later and the gulls get your share!"

"Ha! You can put away enough for three people, easily," she mocked over her shoulder as she swung up her stairway.

"Yes, but when you're eating with me, I always cook enough for six!"

That night she drove the Porsche. They crossed the Currituck Sound Bridge and chose a little-used road on the mainland, and when they ended up near the Virginia border, Kiel suggested they keep on in the direction of Norfolk until they found a good restaurant.

"Knowing that the quickest way to your heart is through your stomach," he added with a sardonic smile as she geared down competently to negotiate a narrow, curving bridge.

"Is that what you're aiming for?" she dared, picking up speed again on the straightaway.

"I haven't quite decided yet. Maybe I'm looking for a bedmate, and then again, maybe I'm looking for a good cook . . . you never can tell."

"So when and if you find out, how about letting me in

on it," she quipped, wondering if her sudden shortness of breath were apparent.

Too hungry to search further, they ate at a third-rate diner on juicy, scrumptious hamburgers loaded with big slabs of sweet onions and a horseradish sauce that was unbelievably good. Willy declined beer and settled for milk, to Kiel's disgust. On the way back home, he drove and she snuggled down in the comfort-engineered seat and watched admiringly as he made the powerful pistons march to his tune.

"There's a bit of harshness in the upper midrange, but she's a superb animal for all that," he observed as he slowed down for a stop sign.

"Hmmmm, is that what makes my spine tingle when you let it out? I like it, whatever it is . . . like a huge pipe organ in a tall-ceilinged church."

"You're really a sensuous creature, aren't you, Wilhelmina Silverthorne?" he asked playfully, and she slanted a look at his hawkish profile against the lights of Coinjock Bridge.

"Am I?" she asked. "I suppose so if you mean it in the literal sense."

"I wonder just what else you are?" he mused.

Facetiously, she enumerated on her fingers: "I'm a fairly up-and-coming real-estate saleswoman for one thing and . . . I'm an unbelievably bad violinist for another. Ahhh . . . oh, yes, and I play a near unbeatable game of checkers and . . . and I love ghost stories, especially Ambrose Bierce," she finished with a rush.

He laughed aloud. "The first I wonder about, the second I cringe from, and the third . . . well, I'll challenge you to two out of three anytime you like."

"You're on!" she rejoined gleefully. "And what's

this about doubting my prowess as a salesman—saleswoman if you're into lib jargon?"

"I'm not, and neither are you, thank the Lord. I didn't say you can't make a living at it. You're obviously doing it, but what about those little extras you're so fond of, such as lobsters thermidor and Mercedes sports cars? Don't tell me your commissions cover such luxuries because I won't believe it. No, there's a man somewhere in the background and I'm becoming increasingly curious about him. Feel like taking your hair down, love?"

She remained silent. Kiel's tone had been light and playful, but there was an underlying thread of steel . . . or was it just her imagination? Was she letting past history color present relationships too much? "I feel like taking a nap, is what I feel like taking," she prevaricated, snuggling deeper into her seat and closing her eyes. "If I start talking in my sleep, don't listen; it's only the horseradish talking. It always gives me bad dreams."

"If you start mumbling in your sleep, I'll pull over and listen. I have an idea that what goes on under that lazy, spotted exterior of yours would make mighty fascinating listening."

She hoped he was teasing. Somehow, she sensed a deeper note under his surface lightness, and things were precarious enough without imagining things. She pretended to be asleep until she felt him gearing down for Wimble Court. There was a particular pattern of patches on the pavement that sang against the tires with an unmistakable beat and she sat up and stretched, surprised to find she had really dozed.

Tonight he walked her up her stairs, one arm around her and their hips moving together with a fascinating rhythm as they jostled each other on the narrow treads, and when they reached the top, Kiel took the key from her nerveless fingers and unlocked her door. Before turning on the lights, he revolved her deliberately in his arms, murmured the word, "Onions," and lowered his mouth to her own.

In spite of herself, Willy was caught off guard, for he hadn't kissed her since that night they went dancing, and now she felt all her old fears rushing in on her. Against his intense virility she was utterly helpless, for her own traitorous body negated the warnings of her cautious mind. As his kiss deepened, probing, tasting, provoking her into a response, her arms went around his waist and her fingers dug into the satin-hard muscles of his back, and he groaned and hauled her breathlessly close to him, making her alarmingly aware of his aggressive masculinity. Taking the lobe of her ear into his mouth, he breathed her name over and over and each stroke of his breath on her sensitized nerves brought her closer and closer to surrender.

One of his hands moved up to her breast and she curved into the pressure, craving it as a starving man craves food, while deep inside her some flickering fragment of rationality told her she was courting disaster. She had been hurt badly enough, the voice of sanity whispered, when only her pride had been involved, but what if more were concerned in this case? Kiel Faulkner was a man apart, a man whose natural dominance had nothing to do with what he owned, but with what he *was,* and any sexual entanglement with a man of his caliber could only spell disaster.

Even as her frantic mind sent messages of caution, her willful body was growing more and more lethargic, its senses drugged with the sweet narcotic of passion.

Her hands slid slowly down his sides to his hips, digging into the hard muscles convulsively in a way that had an immediate physiological effect on him as a man.

"God, Willy, I want you so much I'm going out of my mind! You— Come on," he growled, half-dragging her in the direction of the bedroom.

"No . . . Kiel, no," she pleaded in a last-ditch effort to slow the lemminglike course of self-destruction.

"What is it?" he demanded hoarsely, reaching down to lift her in his arms as if she weren't five feet, eight inches of solid woman.

"Kiel, I can't—I mean I . . . I don't . . ." she faltered, wrapping her arms around his neck because she felt totally, illogically secure in his arms.

"God, what is this?" he exclaimed unbelievingly. "Don't tell me I've got my signals crossed because I'm no inexperienced boy, Willy. You want it just as much as I do, and that's saying a lot. Come on, darling, I can take care of you, if that's what you're worried about." His voice had dropped to a low rumble that made gooseflesh rise on her spine and she wondered frantically if she had strength of character enough to hold out against both of them.

"Kiel, please put me down," she whispered into his warm, pulsating throat. "I . . . I don't think I'm ready for this sort of an involvement."

She could feel his eyes burning into her soul in the still darkness about them, and sense the hardening withdrawal in spite of his still-ragged breathing. The arm that supported her knees released her abruptly so that she staggered, and he steadied her only briefly before removing his arm from her shoulders. His voice was a raw parody of itself: "I'm a little old for this sort of game, Willy. If you grow up anytime soon, let me know; otherwise, I'll see you around."

And then he was gone, leaving her staring blindly at the cool diffusion of moonlight through the screen-covered door. What had happened to the warm, comfortable friendship that had sprung up between them so spontaneously? Had it only been physical on his part? Something so superficial and fragile that it fractured irreparably when he ran up against her last line of defense? How could she be joking about something so ridiculous as onions and horseradish one moment and then be shaken by sarcasm, bruised by animosity the next?

For animosity it was; there had been no mistaking that hard bitterness that radiated from him when he put her down so abruptly, nor the sarcasm in his final words.

Willy turned away slowly and fumbled for the light switch. This time she pulled the shades, not caring to have any interested bystander see her when she dropped to the couch and buried her face in her hands. There were no tears. No, she was a big girl now, in spite of Kiel's insinuations, and she wouldn't give him the satisfaction of knowing he could make her cry.

For the first time in ages, Willy was on time the next day. The night had brought with it little rest and she surveyed the overcast sky through her salt-smeared window with a baleful feeling of satisfaction. She could not have stood the false cheer of a brilliant sun today, and if she wanted to wallow in morose self-pity for a few hours—hours that *would* have been spent in a brisk swim and a shared breakfast while they argued amiably over the pages of the *Virginian Pilot*—then what difference did it make, as long as she presented a cheerful facade at work? She could do without speculation in that quarter.

Dotty greeted her with the news that Matt wanted to see everyone in his office at nine-fifteen, and she frowned in fierce concentration at the scribbly appointment calendar on her desk, seeing among her compulsive doodlings the reminder that she was showing a house in Colington at ten.

"You look like you could do with a vacation," Dotty observed. "Been burning the candle?"

"I tried jogging after an early-morning swim lately. Didn't I tell you exercise was hazardous to the health?"

"Ha, ha!" the secretary mocked. "The day you exercise to the point of heavy breathing will be a long time coming, Willy Silverthorne, so pull the other one."

"The Chiswicks. Haven't I heard that name before?" Willy speculated, glad to leave the subject of her recent activities. "I'm showing them that place at Colington this morning. Any advice?"

"Only that if they're the same Chiswicks who were in here off and on for the past month, Pete's already shown them half the county. I think they're sightseers, taking advantage of a free ride and a guided tour."

Groaning, Willy got up and poured herself a cup of coffee, staring out the window at the CCE Building as she sipped it, and then, with an exasperated exclamation, she put down her cup and marched into Matt's office. Each of the three men rose when she entered and both Pete and Frank offered her their chair, but she smiled and took a perch on the corner of a low filing cabinet, absently picking dead leaves off Matt's begonia.

Half an hour later, the three of them stood morosely, after having had their own observations confirmed. When the two men filed out of the office, Matt signaled Willy to remain behind. He closed the door, then returned to lean against his own desk with a frown marring his nice, regular features. "It's all too true, you know, Willy. Economic ups and downs, interest rates, gas uncertainties—it all adds up to a slowdown in business. Meanwhile, overhead goes up at a rate that makes my head swim." He shook his head as if to illustrate his point.

Seeking to smooth out the worry lines on his young-old face, Willy murmured something to the effect that where there were people there would always be a need for housing and not only on a temporary basis. "Second homes are our stock-in-trade, I know, Matt, but look how many newcomers are flocking down here to live. Ada Willits, who lives downstairs from me, said her parents lived out the depression here on collards and croakers, so maybe we should change our focus."

He grinned, some of the worry leaving his eyes. "Okay, Pollyanna, point taken. All the same, I thought you should know which way the wind's blowing."

"Just so it blows. My air-conditioner's been on the blink for three weeks and the man keeps telling me he'll get to it terreckly, whatever *that* means."

"Then why don't we go out to a nice air-conditioned restaurant and maybe take in whatever's playing at the Colony House afterward?"

On the point of making an excuse, Willy impulsively agreed. It was just the medicine she needed to keep her mind off Kiel Faulkner. When you get thrown, the best thing to do is to get right back on again, she thought, then immediately began picking holes in her rationale. As if Matt or any other man could take her mind off Kiel.

It was almost ten and she had to meet the Chiswicks at their motel at ten, so she asked if she might borrow the station wagon.

"When are you going to get yourself a sensible car, Willy?" Matt asked, strolling out with her. "Let me get something out of the glove compartment and it's all yours."

They stood there in the parking lot for several minutes while Matt went over the points she needed to stress about the Colington place, and then, as she slid under the wheel, he called after her, "I'll be out all afternoon, so why don't you just keep this and I'll drive yours and we'll meet at the Drake at eight?"

Since Matt lived at Southern Shores, and Willy all the way at the other end of the beach, in South Nags Head, they usually both drove to save time and gas. Willy tossed him her keys, trusting his ultraconservative driving habits, and backed out of the shady parking place and only then did she see Kiel standing outside the CCE offices. He had just turned away from talking with two men who carried rolled-up drawings as if they were priceless manuscripts and now he paused in the act of opening the door and stared at her. Neither of them acknowledged the other, but Willy had the unmistakable feeling that he had been aware of her the whole time she had been talking to Matt and she lifted her chin imperceptibly. Wasn't this just what she wanted, to let him know that she didn't have to tumble into bed with the first man who kissed her? She wasn't that much of a pushover, no matter how devastatingly attractive the man was.

Her foot hit the floorboards in a vain effort to clutch and she swore mildly at all automatic transmissions for preventing people from expressing themselves on the road, and then she grinned ruefully at the self-image *that* thought conjured up. Anyone would think she was a teenage boy with his first hot rod, when actually she simply enjoyed one of the few luxuries that remained to her.

And unless she got on the ball and sold something to someone soon, even that luxury would go by the board. Upkeep and maintenance on a car like her little persimmon were not cheap.

The Chiswicks were a charming couple, retired and boasting of fourteen grandchildren scattered all over the country. While Willy sat in the car and waited for them to explore the Wright Memorial and the nearby museum—"Since we're passing so close, I'm sure you won't mind, my dear"—she thought sourly that in a world whose greatest problems stemmed from overpopulation, fourteen grandchildren weren't so much to be bragged about but to be apologized for, and then her natural good nature came to the surface again and she damned the man who had put her out of sorts toward all mankind today, and set herself out to be charming to the prospective buyers, knowing all along that they weren't really interested in buying anything more than a morning's entertainment.

They walked around the tall frame house, with its oddly hopeful look, and Willy pointed out the cistern that was no longer needed for water and the Dorothy Perkins roses, their tiny leaves frosted with mildew, and tried to remember just what it was Matt told her to stress. They strolled through the empty house, their footsteps echoing hollowly, and when Mrs. Chiswick murmured something about the graciousness of high ceilings, Willy told her gently that the heating system was as old as the house itself, and when Mr. Chiswick remarked on the large, multipaned windows, she mentioned the winds that blew in off the sound in the wintertime, making storm windows almost a must.

At twelve-fifteen, she left them at their motel. They thanked her for a lovely morning and she smiled at them warmly and kicked herself for being a fool.

Lunch was a quick milk shake, and she stayed busy, both in the office and out of it, until almost six. When she let herself out the back door, locking up after herself, there was only one car left in the lot besides the station wagon. Kiel Faulkner stood talking to the woman who had been Randy's secretary and was now his, she supposed, and as they were between the two vehicles, there was no way she could ignore them.

"Willy, you know my secretary, don't you?" Kiel asked blandly. "Claudia Dunn, Wilhelmina Silverthorne. Claudia used to work for Collier before he left, as you might know."

As I might know, Willy repeated irritably in her mind. Her smile was slow in coming and probably not very gracious, but the sleek brunette, looking as flawlessly groomed as if she hadn't been working eight and a half hours, didn't even make the effort. They had never had much use for each other, since it was no secret that until Willy came on the scene, Claudia Dunn was all set to parlay a working relationship into something much more.

"You mentioned the Drake," Kiel said. "Is it any good?"

Rolling down the windows of the station wagon to allow the steam to escape, Willy told him grudgingly that it was average.

"I can't see you settling for a place that's only average," he taunted, looking unfairly cool and unflappable in spite of the sultry heat that bore down on them through a brassy gray sky.

"It does a pretty good clam chowder and I suppose their lemon chess pie is as good as any you'll find," she conceded.

"Sounds promising," he said to his secretary. "You interested?"

Willy didn't wait to hear the answer. She slammed her door and reversed smoothly out of the slot, thankful for once that she didn't have any gears to grind because it would be just her luck to do something stupid with those two for an audience.

Matt was late. Willy had been determined to meet him outside and insist on going somewhere else, but by the time he pulled into the crowded lot, she was starved, and he was so apologetic that she hadn't the heart to suggest they go somewhere else. Besides, knowing Matt, he had made reservations in advance. He always played it safe.

What the hell! The parking lot was jammed and there was no silver-gray Porsche; it would serve him right to come roaring up here only to find there was no room either inside or outside. And there, like a thumbed nose, would be her persimmon-colored Mercedes, and . . .

Oh, Willy! How childish can you get? she ridiculed. As if it mattered one whit to Kiel Faulkner where she ate her dinner!

The clam chowder was too peppery tonight, the hush puppies were dry, and they were out of lemon chess pie. Besides which, Matt was hinting around about one breadwinner in a family being enough and what did she think of raising a family while they were young enough to enjoy them instead of waiting until they thought they could afford them. She asked what was playing at the Colony House and then pretended an interest she was far from feeling. All she wanted to do now was to get out before Kiel and Claudia showed up, which she was sure they would do, and before Matt became more explicit.

They almost made it. Willy was studying the geodetic survey charts on the wall of the minuscule lobby while Matt paid the check and they turned to go out just as Kiel opened the door for Claudia . . . a Claudia, Willy noticed with intense distaste, who was clinging like a barnacle and laughing up in his face as if he were the cleverest man on the face of the earth.

"Oh, hello, you two," Kiel greeted. "How was dinner?"

Irritated by his bland urbanity, Willy told him shortly that the chowder was too peppery and they were out of lemon chess pie.

"I can't stand clam chowder, anyway," Claudia asserted, as if only a person of low breeding could, "and they're sure to have vanilla ice cream."

Kiel, holding the door for them, said in a low voice as Willy brushed past him, "Personally, I enjoy a taste of spice, and as for dessert, well, I prefer to improvise . . . later."

"What was that all about?" Matt wanted to know as he saw her to her own car.

"Oh, nothing, he was just passing a smart-aleck remark. Meet you at the theater, all right?"

The picture was as dry as the hush puppies had been and completely lacking in spice, and by the time Matt saw her to her car again, Willy was yawning widely.

"I don't suppose you'd care to go for a drive," he suggested wistfully, and Willy thought, For a drive or parking? Matt lived with a married couple and had no place of his own to take a date. So far, he had done little more than hint that he wouldn't mind spending an evening at Willy's apartment and she had put him off, instinctively shying away from a deeper involvement with a man she knew could never be more than a friend.

"I'm bushed, Matt. Today was more than I bargained for, and unless you want me trailing in about noon tomorrow, you'd better let me go home while I can still keep my eyes open." She grinned sleepily and, on impulse, leaned over and kissed him lightly on the corner of the mouth. "It was nice, Matt. I didn't need the pie, anyway. Remind me to bring you a sample of my own lemon chess pie."

"*You*'re nice, " he replied gallantly, "and if I weren't your boss as well as your date, I might argue with you. Good night, honey. Drive carefully."

She did—carefully, slowly and far too thoughtfully, seeing Claudia hanging on to Kiel's arms, her usually composed face alive with frank interest. There were no lights on in Kiel's house when she pulled up close beside her own apartment and she wondered if he were home yet. Was alone? Were they parked somewhere watching the moon rise over the ocean, laying out a silver carpet before it? Or were they over there across the way, lying on the cushioned lounge, having a dessert of wine and cheese?

Willy was almost asleep when the first strains of music drifted through her open window, and when she recognized the haunting strains of an aria from *The Pearlfishers,* she pounded her pillow furiously and then pulled it over her head.

Chapter Four

For the next few days, Willy saw nothing of Kiel and she hated to admit, even to herself, how badly she missed him. That brief period when she had seen him several times a day could almost have occurred in another lifetime, so isolated did it seem now in the oppressive heat of summer doldrums. She found herself snapping at Pete and Frank when they teased her and even Dotty came in for her share of Willy's ill humor.

"I want to know what in the world has happened, Willy," Dotty demanded one day when Willy spilled a folder and proceeded to tell the office at large what she thought of trying to manage without a file clerk. "Somebody's put your nose out of joint and I'm warning you, honey, unless you come around pretty soon, you're going to make the post office's least-wanted list. Even Richy was complaining about your moping upstairs all the time."

"Oh, golly, am I as bad as all that?" Willy shoved her hair back from her face and grimaced. "It's the heat. Dog days, isn't it?"

"Nope, not yet. We still have that to look forward to."

"Where'd you see Richy, anyway? I haven't seen either him or Ada since she started working nights at the convenience store."

Dotty rolled a sheet of paper in her typewriter and adjusted it. "He's signed on with Bill for the Blue Marlin Tournament. They've gone to Hatteras for the duration and he's probably going to work as mate until he goes back to school." Dotty's boyfriend, Bill Yancey, was skipper of a fishing boat that carried out sports fishing parties in the summertime and did commercial fishing during the winter. He was a nice-enough man but Willy had never heard him say more than two consecutive words.

"You planning to go down to join them?" Willy asked.

"Nope. I'm still determined to bone up and take my realtor's exams whether I ever work at it or not. Just to prove to myself that I can. Then, and only then, will I settle down and raise a houseful of little Bills." She grinned and Willy was struck by the thought that some people didn't know how lucky they were.

And then she shook herself out of her maudlin sentimentalism. Kiel Faulkner was no more husband material than she herself was wife material. She had seen little enough of marriage that appealed to her, and certainly not the examples closest home, where her father seemed determined to pick up where Ponce de León left off, using younger and younger mates as the magic elixir.

The next morning she was thanking the Lord it was Friday as she descended the stairs, fumbling in her handbag for her keys, when Kiel greeted her with the news that his car wouldn't start. "How about a lift to work?" he asked.

Disconcerted, she nodded. "Sure. Hop in. What is it, the battery?"

70

"Nothing so mundane, I'm afraid. I'll check it out later when I have more time, but just now I want to finish up at the office in time to get off early and head down the banks."

She shot him a questioning look, concentrating on her driving with more difficulty than usual as she became aware of the subtle scent of his aftershave, the casual spread of his powerful thighs in the seat beside her.

"Blue Marlin Tournament. I thought I'd take a break and go down to watch the start. I need an offshore breeze to blow the office dust out of my brain."

"You're going in a boat, then?"

He laughed briefly. "I don't walk on water. You're interested in boats?" He had heard the spark of interest in her voice, but it was Kiel she was interested in, not his mode of locomotion for a change.

She acknowledged a slight interest as well as an even slighter knowledge. "Daddy was always certain I'd trip and fall overboard, or so he said, but I found out later he just didn't want any big-eyed, big-eared little pitchers around," she said ruefully, wondering immediately why she had volunteered anything about her past.

"Your father sailed, then? Around here, by any chance?"

Full stop. She didn't intend to say any more about her home or her family and so she pointed out a hang glider getting ready to launch himself from the top of Jockey's Ridge, and the moment passed.

"Park it in the shade today," Kiel offered with a glint of humor in his metallic eyes. "In case I need to catch a ride back down the beach with you later on, I don't want to bake."

"Such selfless consideration overwhelms me," she derided.

Kiel walked with her to the place where the ramp split to go to the separate buildings. "Since I'm grounded today, may I take you to lunch?"

"Why don't you just ask if you can borrow my car and be done with it? Or is this more of your selfless consideration?" she gibed.

"It wouldn't occur to you to impute a higher motive to my invitation, would it?" he asked dryly.

She regarded him skeptically for a minute, and then, surrendering to her own self-interest, she agreed. "All right, since you're afoot today, I suppose it would be practical."

"Practicality wasn't quite the motive I had in mind, Miss Silverthorne, but if you feel you have to rationalize, then be my guest. I'll see you at about twelve-thirty."

He veered off with a brief wave and a sardonic lift of eyebrow and Willy instantly regretted her weakening. The man was infuriating! Smug, arrogant, utterly certain that all he had to do was snap his fingers and any woman within range would fall victim to his lethal charm! "I could always bring you a corndog and a Twinkie," she called after him, and he turned without breaking stride and said, "Twelve-thirty!"

She swore she wouldn't. All morning long, between two-finger typing and answering the phone, she told herself she'd cut her losses and do herself a real favor; but when twelve-twenty passed, she stood up, stretched and strolled aimlessly to the rest room, where she scrutinized her image in the well-lighted mirror.

Oh, Lordy, what kind of fool would try and match *this* against Claudia's magnolia skin, her midnight-blue eyelashes and that irritating knack she had of staying perfectly groomed no matter what the weather? *This* being a perennial crop of freckles, a mop of hair that usually resembled a haystack, with matching brows and lashes, and a way of coming undone even before she got to work in the first place. Sure, there was nothing wrong with the actual shape of her face, or her nose, or her chin or her cheekbones, for that matter, and her eyes were large enough, even if their cloudy green color was half-covered by a positive hedge of colorless lashes, but her clothes. . . . Without a maid to direct her wardrobe from start to finish, Willy had rapidly deteriorated to the point where she threw on something cool and cotton and let it go at that, although lately she had tried to make amends, conscious of the fact that she wanted Kiel to look on her with favor.

Oh, phoo! It was too much trouble and she wasn't going to start going to a lot of trouble for any man! Certainly not for one who'd only laugh at her if he had any idea of how much it mattered to her. If she couldn't attract a man without her father's money glowing behind her like a twenty-four-karat-gold halo, then she'd do without.

With a last half-mocking glance in the mirror, she pushed open the door and returned to the open office, to see Kiel leaning casually against Dotty's desk chatting as if they were bosom buddies. He looked up and smiled blandly. "Ready to go?"

She nodded, and as he held the door open for her, he turned to Dotty and said, "Think about it, will you? I'll talk to you after lunch."

"What was that all about?" Willy asked as she fumbled for her dark glasses. In spite of an overall haze, the light was fierce.

"Tell you over lunch."

She handed over her keys and told him to drive and he made a big show of being shocked, asking her if she' was sure she trusted him.

"With my car, yes."

"That one was below the belt," he charged, and then added, "and that was no deliberate double entendre."

She shot him a swift look that almost immediately crumpled into a grin, disarmed by the amusement she saw reflected in his lean face. Lowering himself under the wheel after seeing her seated, he extracted the Mercedes from between its companions with an economy of movement that was a joy to watch and Willy reminded herself forcefully that if she didn't look out, she'd be right back where she was before.

She didn't ask where they were going, content to feel the speed-induced wind comb through her hair, and to watch the beautiful precision of his hands as they handled the gears with a finger-light touch. Those hands, she thought with wry honesty, were as expert at directing a piece of machinery as they were at directing the reactions of a woman's body, and heaven help her if she forgot that fact!

They ate at the same small, unimposing beachfront place where he had taken her that day with Kip and they vied with white-haired surfers for space. Kiel ordered the soft-shell crab sandwiches with beer for himself and milk for her and he frowned as he replaced the spotted menu in its holder. "I don't think Moses would have approved of your having milk with shell-fish," he told her.

"Probably not, but let's hope this place has better sanitation and refrigeration facilities than Moses did."

"As a health officer at a time when one slipup could be fatal, he did a first-class job of getting his people through safely, but I'll bet he never saw a crab sandwich that could compare with these," Kiel said, accepting their order from a waiter whose T-shirt read simply, T shirt.

They talked of food and its preservation in a variety of climates, and Willy gradually relaxed her wariness and found herself laughing wholeheartedly for the first time in a week, but when Kiel said, "If you'll wipe off that milk mustache, I've a proposition to put to you," she stiffened again.

He reached across the table and wiped her mouth with his napkin, the sun creases around his eyes deepening. "On Dotty's behalf, that is," he added. He went on to explain that Dotty was down in the dumps because Bill was going to have to celebrate his birthday without her. "He's registered in the tournament and he left for Hatteras this morning and won't be home until next weekend. It occurred to me that since I plan to sail down for the weekend to watch the start, Dotty might like to come along as a passenger and then she and Bill could have a little celebration after he winds things up Saturday night. Of course, it all hinges on having another woman along. What about it, are you game?"

"Who, me?" she asked awkwardly. "You mean leave today?"

"Why not? Here, come on outside. I can't hear a thing over that demolition derby they call music." He steered her through the crowd around the jukebox and they paused on the sagging porch to gaze out over an empty lot that was aglow with yellow flowers.

75

"What about it?" he murmured absently as he looked out over the flowers to where cloud shadows chased themselves across the solemn dome of Kill Devil Hill. "Looks as if the weather's going to cooperate."

A nameless sort of excitement started somewhere down inside her and tightened up her throat so that she had to try twice before she could get her words out. "Does . . . does Dotty really want to go? I thought she was busy studying for her realtor's exam. She and Bill plan to be married as soon as she passes."

Kiel lighted a narrow cigar and blew a stream of smoke out into the sunshine. "She can always study aboard the *Good Tern* while Bill's working."

"The *Good Tern*. That's your boat, I suppose."

He ushered her down to where the persimmon-colored car held its own against a flock of rusty beach buggies, landscaped vans and neon-colored custom jobs. "My first one was named the *Royal Tern*. A bit ostentatious, but then, one's first boat . . ." He shrugged as if to excuse a perfectly understandable touch of pride.

"You traded it in on this one?" She winced and slid her hands under her as the hot leather branded her thighs.

"It was a casualty, I'm sorry to say. My . . . my half-brother borrowed her for a cruise with friends and someone got careless with refueling. Fortunately, no one was hurt and Ra . . . my brother lost his taste for sailing. At any rate, I decided one good tern deserved another, thus the name, and if you say it's cute, I'll swat you where you're sitting down."

"Oh, definitely not cute. A bit glib . . . facetious, perhaps, but certainly not cute." She gurgled as he reached out and made good his threat, catching her on the side of the leg.

By the time they returned to the offices it was decided that, Dotty being agreeable, they'd meet at Oregon Inlet at four and plan to be under way as soon after as possible, allowing them plenty of time to reach Hatteras and get a good night's sleep. Then, early on Saturday before the boats went out, they'd contact Bill and make arrangements to get together after he came in that evening. They'd watch the beginning of the tournament, which officially began on Sunday, although there'd be a lot of activity on Saturday as well, and make their way back home late on Sunday afternoon.

It was just after two when Willy left the office. Kiel had called to say that he'd arranged for his car to be taken care of and would see her at home about three-thirty. Several times she had almost succumbed to second thoughts. Second and third and even fourth ones, but Dotty's excitement was contagious; and when she asked herself, Why not? she carefully avoided listening for an answer.

The Porsche was miraculously cured of its ailment—something esoteric that Kiel explained away with a few words, none of which Willy understood—and they loaded it with two ice chests he had ready and waiting. Her own flight bag held a change of clothes plus a few incidentals, and Kiel evidently kept a supply of things aboard his boat, because except for the comestibles, he went empty-handed.

They parked her Mercedes in his garage before setting off and Willy's feeling of exhilaration grew as they passed Bodie Island Light and headed on down toward the marina at Oregon Inlet. The campground on the other side of the highway was bustling with activity and the marina, with half its boats still out and others cruising in sight near the high, arching bridge, was a beehive. Dotty was waiting, looking out of place in a cotton dress and perfectly unaware of the fact. They moved on to one side where a small tender was moored, and after loading it, Kiel rowed them out to where a sleek handsome ketch of some thirty-five or forty feet was moored.

The *Good Tern* was glistening white fiberglass with a teak stern that designated her registry as Bar Harbor, Maine, a fact which caused Willy to reflect on how very little she knew about Kiel Faulkner, but he was busy preparing to get under way, and by the time the provisions had been stowed aboard and Dotty had finished exclaiming over everything in sight, the moment had passed.

They went out under bare poles, in water that caught the glint of a late sun, silhouetting dozens of small boats against a pale-gold haze. Kiel explained that the channel wasn't wide enough to negotiate comfortably under sail with the wind in that quarter but that once they gained deep water off the northern end of Hatteras Island, he'd hoist sail.

Willy didn't care. She was unreasonably happy, almost choked with a sort of expectant joyousness, and she told herself firmly that she was only along because Dotty needed another woman with her and Dotty was only along because Kiel had planned to make the trip anyway.

So don't build on it, my girl, she warned herself sternly. She had no trouble finding her way about, for she had known a few harbor sailors who used just such yachts for entertaining, seldom, if ever, leaving port. She had gone to several yacht parties with Luke and Jasper until Jasper began to notice the attention she received from his male friends, and then the invitations had suddenly stopped coming. Which suited her just fine. Hard-drinking, poker-playing, wife-swapping sophisticates weren't her idea of good company, anyway, and she had been slightly surprised that Luke went along with the crowd. Of course, that was before she understood that he was Jasper's hired man.

Enough of the past, she told herself, making her way up forward to sprawl facedown on a sun-warmed deck. It felt good on her bare skin, the contrast between hot teak and cool breeze with a hint of spray thrown in for added zest. She had sailed in small boats when she was younger, but nothing in this class. When Kiel cut the engines and hoisted the main, she rolled over onto her back and raised her arm to shade her face, gazing up in rapt admiration. The sight of all that translucent white dacron against a deep blue cloudless sky was enough to bring tears to the surface of her eyes and she chided herself for a silly fool.

But then Willy also cried at parades and airports, something that had driven her father wild. He had no use for tears, calling all the softer emotions sloppy sentimentalism; however, she supposed one didn't harness the amount of power and wealth Jasper Silverthorne had by indulging in weaknesses.

Why did she keep on thinking of her father? She sat up and shoved impatient fingers through her hair. It must be the yacht and the fact that she was back again in the rarefied atmosphere of money after months of living on a tight budget, learning to love her shabby, makeshift furniture. Surprisingly enough, she had not once missed the quiet elegance of her father's home, where everything moved on well-oiled wheels. There had always been a uniformed figure hovering in the background of her life, in case a Silverthorne wanted something, and she could remember from the time she was six, when Jasper—he had been Daddy then—had moved her there with his second wife . . . she remembered being driven down that long, curving driveway between double rows of white-boled royal palms. It had been a Corniche and the chauffeur's name had been Astin and he had never smiled. She remembered that.

She had been Mina then. Little Mina Silverthorne, Jasper's homely little heiress, made much of by his women friends until she had suddenly shot up to her full height; then she was kept in a succession of expensive, cloistered establishments until she had outgrown them as well.

That had all ended quite suddenly when she had discovered that she had a will to match her father's, and since he was in no position to argue, with his latest marriage on the line, she had had her own way and now she discovered that she quite enjoyed cooking her own meals, swatting her own mosquitoes and strolling into a waterfront café to see the admiring glances cast her way.

"From wistfulness to grim determination to smug satisfaction; what *is* causing that remarkable array of expressions, I wonder?" Kiel asked from directly above her. His deck shoes had made no sound and now she looked up to see that he had changed into navy trunks and a white windbreaker. The glowing ball of sun turned his skin copper.

"Maybe I'm just hungry," she suggested lazily, smiling up through a curtain of hair.

"You know what has to be done, then, unless you'd care to take the helm while I do the honors."

She sat up with a graceful economy of movement. "Not unless you want to be painting *Good Tern the Third* on another transom."

"Warning duly noted. Actually, she'll sail herself in all but the most extreme conditions, but I'd as soon not risk it as we near the cape. Pity you won't be able to see the stream in the dark, but we'll see it tomorrow and Sunday."

"Want to hear something silly? I always thought we owned the Gulf Stream . . . we Floridians, that is." She took the hand he extended to her and stood up, finding herself altogether too close to him.

"So you're from Florida originally. Then chances are you've sailed before?"

He made it a question but she refused to be drawn. "Small-boat stuff," she allowed, dropping down into the cockpit and making her way below.

Dotty raised her head and slid her glasses back up on her nose. "Getting about time to eat, isn't it? I can't see to read much longer, anyway."

"I don't see how you can go on reading down here without getting sick as a dog," Willy said, opening the compact refrigerator to see what Kiel had provided.

"I've got a cast-iron stomach."

"You're telling me!" Willy cracked. She had lunched with her friend often enough to deplore the consumption of cardboard sandwiches and plastic desserts washed down by quarts of cola.

The refrigerator held a treasure trove and Willy

decided to try something simple for her first shipboard attempt: filet of beef with parsley potatoes and a simple salad with a really good dressing. Calling up the companionway, she asked Kiel his choice of wine to go with the steaks and then located the French red he suggested. There was a creamy Italian Mezzanello for afterward, and she shaved off a sliver and put it in her mouth as she went about familiarizing herself with the ingenious cooking facilities.

By the time they came abreast Cape Hatteras Light, the sky was like diamond-studded black velvet and Kiel announced his decision to anchor in the bight until the next morning. "I don't particularly want to try Hatteras Inlet at dead low tide, and besides, we'll be a lot more comfortable out here with a breeze than we would on the inside in the lee of the island."

Dotty cleaned up after the meal as her share, still effusing over what she called the cutest kitchen. She said she wanted to get to bed so she could be up extra early in the morning, and so Kiel showed her how to arrange the shower wall and assured her that there was plenty of fresh water.

Exploring the teak and holly counter and the clever storage compartments, Willy had discovered a supply of tapes and a deck, and so she had selected several of her favorites and put them on. An hour or so later, the last one ended while she and Kiel were relaxing on the two outside benches, and now there was only the creak of the rigging to break the stillness of the night. By the intermittent sweep of light from shore, Willy watched Kiel's silhouetted profile, reading in it a strength and toughness that was not as apparent when one was distracted by his surface attractiveness. Again she was reminded that this was a man, not a boy to be put off with a smile and a teasing kiss.

"Sleepy?" he asked, his voice keyed to the unearthly beauty of the night.

"Not really," she replied as softly. "Know what I'd love to do? Go swimming."

"Now?"

"Mmmmhmmmm. Could I?"

"Au naturel?"

She caught her breath. "If you mean in the raw, then no, thanks. I don't think it's really wise, do you?"

"Swimming at night never is, no matter what the circumstances," he replied dryly. "Go put on your suit."

Perversely, she reminded him, "We've just eaten."

"Over an hour ago. Besides, I'll stick with you. You're not a very energetic swimmer at the best of times, are you?"

"You know me," she drawled, ambling the few feet to the door of the cabin she was to share with Dotty. "If there's a wave, I'll ride it; if not, I'll float."

By the time she was ready to go over the side, it looked terribly dark and she hung back, thinking of all the things that could be lurking under the surface. This was no safe pool, with Astin standing by with his chrome-plated rod.

"Second thoughts?" came the mocking baritone behind her.

She took a deep breath and dived, coming up from the surprisingly warm water in time to see Kiel slice through without a splash several yards away. He joined her then as she trod water and suggested a leisurely swim around the hull as a constitutional, and she tried and failed to suppress a rising sense of excitement. She eased into a slow, graceful Australian crawl, a stroke that she had discovered to be much less energetic, and he kept pace with her, his leg occasionally brushing against her own.

They went around the darkly gleaming hull twice, swimming under bow and stern lines, and when, winded and laughing, she caught at the boarding ladder, Kiel swam up beside her and reached around to cover her hand with his. The move brought him in bodily contact with her and she felt the buoyant saltwater float her feet up so that her legs tangled with his and he caught her in a scissors grip and turned her to face him, keeping them both afloat with one hand on the ladder.

"You exerted yourself too much," he murmured against her dripping hair. "Your heart's about to jump out of your skin." As if to prove his point, he ran a hand up over her stomach to her breast, not stopping to cup its roundness, but splaying it over her chest so that his fingers touched the base of her throat. Then the hand moved around to the back of her neck, and after a brief fumbling she felt the tension of her bra strings ease. She closed her eyes in silent appeal, knowing she was powerless against the suffocating sensation that was washing away all her resistance. When he untied the strings at her back and she felt her breasts float free on the warm water, she almost sank below the surface and then he tossed the scrap of cloth up into the cockpit and drew her close against the hard length of his body. "My exercise had even more of an effect than yours," he whispered, taking her hand and bringing it up to his chest.

Her fingers combed through the thatch of soft, wet

hair and closed convulsively on the throbbing flesh and then she felt his hands at her hips. "Kiel . . . don't do that!"

"You knew this would happen when you suggested swimming." The words were spoken against her pulsating throat even as he drew away the last barrier of defense and tossed it after her bra.

She began to struggle in his arms, her head lifted frantically above the surface of the water, but her struggles were ineffective because she had to hang on to him to keep from sinking. Warm, vagrant currents swept her legs up between his and he held them there, throwing her far off balance. She was acutely aware of every single movement of his body, both voluntary and involuntary, and when his mouth closed over hers, she was drowning in a sea of sensations.

His tongue seduced her languorously, in tune with the silent currents that swayed their two entwined bodies and she felt her breasts crushed against the sensuous mat that covered his broad chest. She heard the thunder of his heart through her very skin, through her probing nipples, and then, with one arm supporting them both, he allowed the other to stroke through the warm, dark water, sliding over the satiny skin of her back to mold her to him so that there was nothing, no vestige of separation between them, and when he spoke, his voice was a strangled whisper, almost unrecognizable. "God, Willy, help me get you on board or I'll drown us both trying. I've never made love to a woman underwater before, but if you aren't aboard that boat in the next five seconds, I'm warning you, I'm going to do it!"

He lifted her, dragging her agonizingly close to his cool nakedness as he brought her up within reach of the ladder. Her own wet hip brushed against his shoulder and then she was clinging to the rungs as his hand closed over her foot and placed it securely.

"Go, darling . . . hold on now," he cautioned her, and then she was over the side, standing in the starlight with the water streaming down around her and he was poised like some dark nemesis on the rail, devouring her with his eyes.

"You're so unbelievably lovely," he whispered hoarsely as the sweeping beam from the lighthouse limned her naked form. He reached for her and she drew back, overcome by some irrational fear; and when she turned and fled precipitately to the tiny compartment where Dotty lay sleeping peacefully, she leaned against the thin door and heard the accusing silence behind her. And she ached with a terrible longing.

She wanted him; more than anything else in the world, she wanted Kiel Faulkner, not for just a night, but to the edge of beyond; and she knew instinctively that if she gave in to him, that would be the end of it. He had pursued her with the single-mindedness of a man challenged, and once that challenge was gone, he'd be gone as well.

Chapter Five

The crack of sails awakened her and Willy sat up and blinked, completely disoriented for a moment. Then she looked across to see that Dotty's bunk was already made up into its daytime guise. She tossed off the sheet, not unduly surprised to see that she was nude, for on hot, sticky nights, she often slept bare, but as the circumstances of her going to bed returned to her, like the feeling in a limb that's been asleep, she groaned softly and pressed hard against her eyes. Then, wrapping the sheet around her, she padded to the compact head and stared at the hollow-eyed specter in the mirror.

Ten minutes later she felt half-human again. The smell of coffee drifting through the cabin was enough to galvanize her into action and she dressed quickly in white shorts and a navy halter. Stepping into her deck shoes and pulling her hair back carelessly with a cotton bandanna, she pulled back the folding partition and braced herself to face Kiel and pretend that last night had been a swim and a kiss and nothing more.

Anticlimactically, Dotty was alone, sitting at the chart table with her books open before her as she sipped from a steaming mug. "'Morning," she murmured. "Have a good swim last night?"

"Oh, damn," Willy uttered under her breath, turning away to locate a mug. She ate her breakfast silently while Dotty pursued her studies, and finally, when she could no longer fight the dreadful compulsion, she wandered up to the cockpit, studiously looking at the placement of her feet on the well-kept deck. Better to get it over with, she told herself, and since she was such a glutton for punishment, she raised her face deliberately and stared at the man at the helm. He had obviously watched her reluctant approach and now, breaking the ice with a generosity she grudgingly acknowledged, he asked if she'd mind bringing him a mug of coffee.

The hard knot inside her unraveled and she scurried to obey, adding milk and no sugar, as he liked it, and when she retraced her steps to place it carefully in his outstretched hand, he looked her directly in the face, his eyes crinkling into a slow, achingly familiar smile. "I thought we might as well take a run out to the Inner Diamonds since we're this close. Then, if we decide to poke around the village tomorrow instead of following the fleet on out, you won't have missed it."

The atmosphere nicely defused between them, he went on to tell her about the *Lightship* that had been the predecessor to the present *Texas Tower*. "It's called the Graveyard of the Atlantic, but anything less spectral, I've yet to see. Picture a bright red hull with mustard-colored superstructure floating in a royal-blue sea with the shoals flashing like pale emeralds alongside. The first time I saw it, I was barely old enough to see over the sides of the boat, but I've never forgotten it. There was a crewman aboard the *Lightship* playing a bull dolphin on the top of the water and the fish was indescribably beautiful . . . nothing at all like those you see dumped out on the docks when the fishermen bring them in."

"How can anyone stand to catch those creatures, or any other fish, for that matter, and haul them up to drown in the air?"

"That from a girl who can put away two or three big filets at one sitting?" Kiel teased. "The game fish, though, are as often as not just tagged and released." He looked at her and the light on his dark eyes rendered them as opaque as cabochons of hematite. "Do you know what it is to feel the thrill of the chase, Willy? It gets in a man's blood sometimes, but some remnant of humanity allows him to be satisfied with tagging and releasing."

She moved restlessly, watching the billowing sail against the cobalt sky, and then from behind her, his feet bare and braced against the moderate roll of the *Tern*'s deck, Kiel said, "Go on up forward, Willy, and lie down on the bow. If you're lucky you might see a few porpoises or a flying fish." When she moved to obey, needing to get away from his disturbing nearness, he called after her, "Keep one hand on the pulpit stanchion, though. We wouldn't want to lose you."

Feeling almost as if she were one of the flying fish that broke the surface to skim the waves ahead of her, Willy spent most of the next hour watching the hypnotic curl of transparent green water as it parted before the slicing white bow. She saw the incredible colors of the Gulf Stream and the furious shallows of Diamond Shoals some twelve or thirteen miles offshore. After lunch, she sat contented against the main mast and watched the slow trolling of the fishing boats, losing them in the troughs, seeing them reappear again like so many matchbox toys. If anyone caught anything, she wasn't aware of it, nor did she want to know, for in the back of her mind lurked a finger of disquiet when she remembered the words Kiel spoke about tagging and releasing.

She couldn't help but think they had some personal significance and she tried to put them out of her mind as she took the helm and felt for herself the silent power of wind and water. "I could get addicted to this," she said over her shoulder, where Kiel stood watching her.

"I wouldn't be surprised."

Late in the afternoon, as they approached the bell buoy, he got on the radio and raised the *Eldorado* and Dotty spoke to Bill. They arranged for Richy to run out and collect her when they finished up for the day and Willy was left victim to all the familiar tantalizing doubts, knowing she and Kiel would be alone together.

By the time both anchors were out and the standing lights lighted outside the breakwater at Hatteras, the sun had dropped well below the horizon, leaving behind a mirror of clear amethyst with no line of demarcation where sky met water. Against this, the dark mass of Hatteras village lay low and shadowed, with a fringe of white boats along its edge stained with a gold wash by the memory of the sunset. Across the dead calm water came various homey sounds from ashore as well as a drift of hickory-scented smoke from someone's grill. Dotty was monopolizing the head, applying makeup to her pert round face and trying to calm the unmanageable curls that the salt air had sent into violent convolutions.

"My turn to cook tonight," Kiel announced, emerging with two tall, frosty glasses. He had changed into fresh white ducks with a dark red shirt and his hair glistened with wetness from a recent shower.

When Dotty finally came up to await her transportation, Willy took her own shower and changed quickly into the one dress she had brought along, a gauzy cotton caftan of brown, black and white batik. She rejoined the others in the cockpit in time to see Richy roar up and stop just short of the *Tern*. He cut the outboard and greeted them with a wide, toothy grin, and while Dotty went below for still further last-minute preparations, he entertained Willy with the day's happenings, chatting excitedly about the various contestants, some of whom had come from as far away as South Africa.

Kiel watched with what Willy considered unnecessary condescension as the younger man explained the importance of a mate's position in the scheme of things and described in gory detail the sewing on of mackeral and squid for bait. Willy listened indulgently, not because she was interested but because she knew how very fragile Richy's masculine ego was. It was Dotty who broke up the monologue when she asked impatiently if she was expected for dinner aboard the *Eldorado* or should she make herself a sandwich.

"Oh, golly, Skipper'll peel my hide off! He sent over to the fire department fish fry for fish plates and he's probably eaten 'em both by now." He ripped the evening quietness apart with the pull of a rope while Kiel helped Dotty into the tender, and then almost ran into the breakwater when he turned to wave good-bye a third time.

"And I thought *I* was robbing the cradle," Kiel muttered derisively, ducking into the galley to begin dinner preparations.

Almost an hour later, with the scented darkness closing down around her, Willy listened to her stomach rumble and called down the companionway that if he didn't get a move on she was going to fix herself a peanut-butter-and-jelly sandwich.

"Just do that thing," he warned, "and I'll put you out on Oliver's Reef and eat your broiled sturgeon steaks and buttered artichokes myself."

Her bare feet slapped the deck and she pattered down the three shallow steps, looking avidly at the chart table, where two place settings of pewter and ironstone waited to be filled. The two wineglasses of straw-colored liquid were already dewed on the outside and she said plaintively, "I'm starved!"

"Then have a seat and start on this, glutton, and I'll have the sturgeon ready in a minute." He placed a lined pewter bowl before her and she purred at the sight of the delectable petals swimming in a lake of butter.

The meal was eaten to the accompaniment of appreciative murmurs and only when Kiel stood to serve the cheese course and pour small cups of espresso did Willy lean back, replete and marvelously happy. "You're a fantastic cook, Kiel. Where'd you learn?" she asked.

"Picked it up here and there. Why?"

She moved her shoulders in an offhand way under the gauzy covering. "I dunno . . . seems a funny talent for a man of your type."

"Oh?" He finished off the thick black coffee and leveled a sardonic glance at her. "And what talents would you expect of a man of my type?" He put quotes around the last four words.

She grinned lazily at him, far too relaxed to rise to his baiting, and when she answered, her voice was colored with humor. "Things like sailing, of course . . . dancing, probably . . . driving good cars extremely well, and . . . oh, the usual things a practicing playboy goes in for."

"Making love?" he mocked.

"Mmmmm, that goes without saying," she teased.

"If I were a playboy it might."

"And aren't you?"

"I'm a hardworking *man*, with little enough time to *play*, in case you hadn't noticed," he reminded her, lighting a slender cigar and rising to adjust the porthole over his head. The movement brought into relief the beautiful conformation of his muscular arm and she nodded to it.

"You didn't get muscles like those manipulating a slide rule."

His lips curled with what might have been humor. "Are you by any chance hinting for the story of my life?"

"I'm all ears," she purred with overdone eagerness.

"So I noticed when that young sprout was regaling you with the romantic details of sewing baits together and you fell for his line, hook and sinker."

She groaned. "If that's a pun, I've heard better."

"It is, and you haven't," he cracked. "Come on, let's put these things in to soak and get out of here before your adolescent Lothario comes back." He refused her help and she wandered out on deck, inhaling the odd but not unpleasant mixture of gardenias, fish and diesel fuel that drifted out from the shore; and when he came up behind her quietly and placed his hands on her shoulders, she leaned back against the warm solidity of his body as naturally as she drew her next breath.

"The trouble with these compact designs," he murmured against her ear, "is that there's only one place with room enough for two."

She couldn't bring herself to ask, but he told her anyway. "The forward cabin."

Picturing the V berth where Kiel had slept last night, Willy didn't answer, but he must have felt her pulses jump before he went on. "You were about to tell me the story of your life, weren't you?"

At that, she stirred, and he took advantage of the movement to turn her and hold her to him with both arms. "You were about to tell *me*," she corrected.

"What about a trade-off?" He punctuated his suggestion with a kiss on each corner of her mouth and another on the tip of her nose, and when her arms, of their own accord, wound around his neck, his mouth found hers and began a taunting seduction that left her weak and trembling.

"See?" she whispered shakily when he lifted his lips from her soft, wanting mouth, "I told you that went without saying."

"In the vernacular . . . you ain't seen nothin' yet." He rubbed the tip of her nose with his and his soft laughter played on her skin like some exotic breeze, and then he led her to the widest of the two benches and sat down in one corner, drawing her down to lean against him. When she put up her bare feet and snuggled comfortably against his chest, he held her loosely, his hand splaying out on her stomach to burn through the thin stuff of her dress. "All right, begin. You were born, right?"

"You're absolutely right! How clever of you to guess!" she crowed softly, and he flicked his cigar over the side and brought his hand up to capture her chin and turn her face to his.

"Shall I fill in the details for you?" he asked, and she nodded, too affected by his nearness and the scent of coffee, cigar and clean, healthy maleness to do more.

"You were born in Florida . . . central, I'd say,

because you don't strike me as a girl who grew up on the water, yet you're not altogether unfamiliar with it. Let's see . . . father, a doctor, a dentist, or maybe a businessman who spoils his little girl by indulging her taste for pretty cars. Mother . . . ?" He shrugged and Willy felt the play of muscles beneath his dark red knit shirt. "Not a very dominant figure in your upbringing. You show much more influence of men. Sisters? I'd say none, but brothers, perhaps—much older and also prone to indulge in baby sister. How'm I doing so far?"

"It's your story; you tell it."

"All right, now, let's see. Girl comes of age, having conquered every male within range, wants to expand her territory. Dad doesn't like it, but he's a pushover, and so girl sets out on her own and soon finds out she can turn any man she wants to upside down and wrong side out. Can't resist playing little-girl games—lead 'em on, turn 'em off—but still waits for something trophy-sized before bringing out the heavy ammunition. The question is, has she spotted her trophy yet?"

The night air grew chilly and Willy shivered. Suddenly, it wasn't so much fun anymore. She stared broodingly at the fingers that twisted together on her lap.

"Willy? No comment?"

She twitched a shoulder expressively, not knowing what to say without revealing the hurt she felt at his unflattering portrait. Somehow, she hadn't expected him to consider her a mercenary flirt. She said as much.

"Did I say that? I only meant— Well, you have thrown more than a few men for a loop. There's the Willits kid, for one. Hardly legal size, of course, and so you throw him back, but surely there've been a few who qualified as keepers. What about my predecessor at CCE? Someone mentioned that you'd seen a good deal of him."

"Randy?" she exclaimed, startled. "I'd hardly call him a keeper."

"Why not? He was certainly in the keepable income bracket."

"There you go again, insinuating that all I could possibly be interested in is a man's pocketbook! I don't think I like this conversation very much, Kiel," Willy asserted, wrenching herself away from Kiel's arms. She sat huddled over defensively, fighting a demeaning urge to cry.

"Sorry. You must know I'm interested in you, Willy. Maybe I just wanted to make sure I didn't make the same mistake my predecessor made."

"Well, if it's of any interest to you, you did. He—he tried to take me to bed, tried a little too energetically, and—and I hit him and, well, he got angry and called me some not very flattering names and stormed out. Unfortunately, he had been drinking rather heavily before that and he ended up making an even bigger fool of himself by driving into a ditch."

Kiel was silent for so long Willy thought he might not have heard her. He was probably wondering what anyone *could* say to such a sordid little melodrama, short of laughing at it.

"I understood you were seeing him pretty steadily," he said after a while in a voice that sounded almost impersonally disinterested. "Why didn't you want to carry the affair to its logical conclusion? Purely as a matter of interest."

Provoked, she retorted, "Because I didn't love him, not that it's any business of yours!"

"Then why see so much of him in the first place?" he asked with infuriating logic.

She turned to him impatiently. "Good Lord, Kiel, what am I supposed to do, join a convent until a marriage is arranged for me? I like a little social life. I enjoy male companionship—no more, no less than any other red-blooded American girl. Is there something wrong with that? For all I knew, Randy Collier could have been the right man for me. How could I find out without getting to know him better? As it happened, we weren't all that compatible, and when he tried to promote something I didn't want, we broke up. Now, are you satisfied?"

He stood up abruptly and crossed the narrow open space to lean against a stay, gazing out in the direction of the channel marker. They had anchored out in the sound beyond the breakwater because all the spaces along the docks were filled, and now, across the still water came the sound of laughter and a burst of music that was quickly moderated. Willy stared helplessly at the tall, shadowy figure, his legs braced unconsciously against the almost imperceptible motion of the deck, and when he was momentarily revealed by a flash of sheet lightning out over the sound, she could see the rigid set of his shoulders.

She started to speak, clearing her throat and trying again for a light tone. "Turnabout's supposed to be fair play. What about the life and times of Kiel Faulkner?"

After a moment's hesitation, when she thought he hadn't heard her, she turned around to gaze out over the opposite side of the *Tern*, but then he answered her, sounding preoccupied. "It'd bore you, I'm afraid. Maybe we'd better turn in now. I'll do the dishes if you'd like to get through in the head, and then you can have a bit of privacy. Sorry there's not much separation between boudoir and galley."

A surge of disappointment swept over her. "Fine," she said brightly. "It's been a long day, anyway."

Kiel crossed the intervening space with two strides and caught at her arms, pulling her up to shake her slightly; and distraught at the way he seemed to push her from one emotional extreme to another, she cried out, "Kiel, what in heaven's name have I done? Have I said something wrong? Have I offended you in some way? If I have, then I'm sorry, only *tell* me about it! Don't just—just close me out!"

"I don't want to close you out, Willy. Lord help me, I don't want to close you out at all." With those perplexing words, he drew her unresisting figure to him and with an almost awkward sort of urgency, he kissed her.

At first her arms were trapped at her sides and she was torn between wanting to escape the desperate ardor of his kiss and wanting to respond to it. There was nothing of the practiced expert in his lovemaking now; instead, it was almost as if he were kissing her in spite of himself, and she responded instinctively to the raw emotion she felt in him. With a reluctant whimper, she wrapped her arms around his waist and held herself to him with all her strength.

"I think this is when I'd better pour myself a cup of coffee and tell you the unsavory story of my life," he murmured against the hollow of her cheek.

"Who needs the story of your life, stranger? What I need right now is . . ." She proceeded to demonstrate and then, with a sharp intake of breath, he swung her up and moved her to the bench, making room for himself beside her. In the still isolation of the night, she felt his hands on her body, drawing forth a response that left her stunned and breathless. Her words—words born of a glittering sort of wildness that had robbed her of any vestige of responsibility—had pushed him almost too far and now the soft fabric of her loose-fitting caftan proved no barrier to the compelling magic of his hands, and when he moved suddenly and pulled his own shirt over his head, she braced herself for what she knew she had to do.

"Kiel . . ." she began, hating herself, loving him, wanting him yet knowing they were moving too fast. "Kiel, listen to me."

"The time for talking is past, darling. We'll talk later if you insist, but remember, you're the one who said, Who needs the story of your life." He lowered his body onto hers and kissed each eye in turn and she could sense a difference in him, a sort of gentleness that melted her last reserve and she pulled him down and captured his mouth hungrily. They'd talk tomorrow, and if tomorrow never came, she'd have tonight, at least.

"Come on, we'll go inside, darling," he whispered, a febrile light glowing in his dark eyes. "Remind me to trade this tub in on something larger, hmmm?" He stood up and pulled her up with him and she hung there, limp, trembling with eagerness and trying desperately not to think. "Still in the mood for conversation, love? You know what they say speaks louder than words."

He ran his hand down over her shoulders to her waist and over the curve of her hip, and at first, all she could hear was the thunder of two hearts, but then came an intrusive note, a thin, irritating, buzzing sound, and even Kiel stiffened away from her, they heard Richy's voice hailing them from a rapidly narrowing distance.

"My timing leaves a lot to be desired, doesn't it?" Kiel remarked wryly, turning her toward the hatch. "Go below, darling. I won't be a minute."

Before she could disappear, though, Richy roared up and cut the engine, calling out to her in his brash young voice. "Hey, Willy, Dotty says would you get her things together for her and let me take 'em back?"

"What things?" Willy sighed, leaning her hands on the rail as if she lacked the strength to stand, which was not far from the truth.

"I expect he means her night things," Kiel put in.

He did, and by the time Willy had collected Dotty's nightgown, her toilet things and a change of underwear, she felt nothing except an overpowering weariness. She handed them over to the voluble Richy and he took them without even pausing in his recital of the types and weights of billfish that had been taken so far this season.

She turned and made her way below, pulling closed the folding partition that separated her cabin from the narrow companionway. Somehow, she was sure that Kiel wouldn't come after her, and she was right. Long after she had gone to bed, she could hear his movements overhead, and through the porthole came the drift of cigar smoke. She finally fell asleep, more confused than ever, both about her own contradictory feelings and about Kiel's. For someone who was only after a quick conquest, he was showing remarkable restraint. Perhaps he only responded to a challenge, and Lord knows, she had long since ceased to be that!

How could he help but know how she felt when she melted at his very touch? He followed her into her restless dreams, sometimes wearing the face of Matt Rumark and sometimes Randy Collier, and she awoke a few hours later in dead-calm stillness, hot, sticky and thoroughly out of sorts.

Chapter Six

Kiel was doing something to the running rigging and Willy was sipping coffee and waiting for her aspirin to take effect when Dotty returned the next morning. She clambered aboard, her yellow shirtwaist reflecting up on her face to emphasize the expression of almost painful pride there. She had scarcely put both feet over the side before she announced that she and Bill had decided not to wait to get married.

Willy swallowed past an unexpected lump in her throat and embraced her friend, and Kiel offered his best wishes and then busied himself for the next hour or so with a balky halyard winch. When the last of the boats had passed, outriggers bent before the wind as they headed for the fishing grounds offshore, Willy stirred herself and went below to clear away the breakfast things. She had been lying up on the pilot-house, staring out at the channel, but acutely conscious of every move Kiel made as he went about his nautical chores. If he had any thoughts about what had happened the night before, she decided, they had already been relegated to the ranks of the unimportant, for he had greeted her over the breakfast table as naturally as if she were in fact a passenger brought along for the convenience of Dotty Sealy.

When, after testing the winch and finding it running smoothly once more, Kiel suggested that they go ashore and stretch a few legs, Willy readily agreed. Here in the close confinement, it seemed that everywhere she roamed brought vivid memories of a kiss or a caress, and she could do without such reminders. Today, Kiel seemed utterly self-sufficient and any small hope Willy had entertained of becoming important to him was fast fading. She didn't seem able to get on his particular wavelength today, for some reason. Gone was the intimate mood when a glance was enough to set off a conflagration.

Dotty declined to accompany them, saying that being on a boat always made her sleepy, and Willy closed the door softly, leaving the small brunette curled up with a beatific smile on her face. Something like envy rolled over inside her and she pushed it away and put on her brightest, most impersonal smile as she joined Kiel in the outboard for the short run into the harbor.

Hatteras village had a bright, newly washed look, as if it had rained in the night, although she was certain it hadn't. The talk among the men and boys at the dock was of whose chances were best of beating the 1,142-pound record of the blue marlin displayed at Oregon Inlet.

Strolling through the village, they inhaled the sun-warmed scent of roses, oleanders and the ever-present saltwater tang, and Willy tried to concentrate on the frame houses and small family graveyards tucked in among lush, dark thickets of cedar, yaupon and live oak, with bees droning drunkenly away from the waxy white blooms of yucca. Instead, her peripheral vision admired the way Kiel's well-shaped head rested on his powerful neck and shoulders, the lithe way he had of walking, as if he owned the very earth he trod, and she was glad when he suggested they wander into the library and look through any books about the area. At least there'd be other people there to dilute the concentrated essence of splendid virility he radiated.

The day passed with no uncomfortable undercurrents. On the surface, they were easy companions and they talked comfortably of food and cars and land values in the vicinity, and when after a surprisingly good lunch they made their way back to the docks and out to the *Tern* again, Willy had convinced herself that Kiel was making an attempt to allay any misconceptions about his motives. If he could enjoy her company without once making a pass at her, surely that meant he cared for her?

It was almost with a feeling of anticlimax that Willy watched Kiel raise the anchors and prepare to get under way. She had been lying on deck, drowsing and watching several small boys swimming out from the breakwater after they returned to the *Tern*, and at the hum of the electric motor it came to her that the weekend was over, to all intents and purposes. Had she expected more of it when they set out?

Not really. Lying there now, with her head resting on her hands, she had to admit that although she had begun the trip with a sense of excitement and expectation, there had been no real goal in her mind, nothing she could point at now and say, I accomplished this, or I failed to accomplish that. She stared at the surface of the water, as still and glassy as a mirror, reflecting the small, puffy-dumpling clouds that drifted slowly over the island and out to sea.

Under that deceptive surface were currents and depths that could draw the unwary swimmer down until there was no escape. Like the water flowing under her, Kiel Faulkner was an unknown quantity, and unless she made up her mind to resist that hypnotically attractive surface, she'd surely come to grief by getting in over her head. Like that water, Kiel was deep and rife with forces it was best not to disturb, so why was it that when she was with him, all wisdom deserted her and she was compelled to skirt disaster in spite of all reason?

They went back up the sound instead of going out through Hatteras Inlet again, using the motor rather than the fitful breeze. It was anticlimactic, but then, so was the entire trip, and Willy moved restlessly from bow to stern, inside and out. Dotty was in a mood of dreamy self-containment that precluded any conversation, and Kiel seemed strangely anxious to end the weekend voyage. Probably cutting his losses, she thought defensively, after having failed to get her into his bed. That had been the point of the whole outing, no doubt, and he was disgusted because she had fallen short of his expectations, even as a member of the crew.

And yet, she couldn't quite believe that. He was a complex, difficult man and not one to lay all his cards on the table at this stage of the game, and so she'd just have to play along and hope for the best . . . only she wished she knew just what game it was they were playing.

Oregon Inlet was swarming with small boats. While the tournament might be the big thing for those invited to participate, it was evident that there were plenty who were more than satisfied to try their luck in the waters of the inlet for fish that were less glamorous, but more tasty. Willy had packed her few belongings and stowed away all the food in the ice chests, and now she lay on deck again, enjoying the smooth vibrations and feeling the sun beat down through her jeans and shirt.

Another crop of freckles would be all she had to show for the weekend, she supposed, unlike Dotty, who had taken a step irrevocably into her future.

Kiel was busy with the mooring buoy and Willy supposed she should at least offer to help, but she was half-hypnotized by the sun and the motion, in a sweet, drowsy state when she simply could not compel her limbs to obey her orders.

"You're incredible."

She hadn't even heard his cat-footed approach and now she rolled over on her back and smiled up at him, still caught up in the thrall of her daydreams. "What do you mean?"

"Most women would be lying on a pad annointing themselves with oil and worrying about strap marks and you sprawl here on the deck in rolled-up jeans with your shirt sleeves uneven, collecting half a hundred or so more sunspots without a worry in the world. Where's your vanity, woman?"

She sat up and blinked away a momentary light-headedness, brought on by sleeping in the sun. "That's a low blow . . . I think."

He ruffled her hair playfully and held out a hand, and when she allowed him to pull her to her feet, he caught her lightly against him for just a moment.

Unexpectedly flustered, she hurried into speech. "You know, I just might not have them all year around, now I've left Florida. My freckles, I mean. I'm not sure I'd recognize me all one color."

His grin started in his eyes and spread slowly, crinkling his lean cheeks and the browned skin around his eyes. "You're a nice lady, did you know that, Willy Silverthorne? But you have a way of changing those

106

spots so that a man doesn't quite know what kind of cat he's got hold of."

She looked up at him doubtfully. "I don't think that sounds much like a compliment, but just in case it is, thanks."

Sliding his hands up to her shoulders so as to bring her closer to him, Kiel lowered his face to hers, resting his forehead against her own for just a minute before turning his face so that their lips came together. It was a light kiss—no pressure, no demands—and yet it was that very quality of tentative teasing, the playful feel of those firm-soft lips against her own that disarmed her so completely that it was all she could do not to throw her arms around him and force him to admit that whatever it was between them was more than mere physical attraction.

The tension built until it was a palpable thing, and then he lifted his face and gazed down at her searchingly, and she was once more thoroughly confused by what she read in his eyes.

"Kiel?" she whispered tentatively.

"Time to go." He turned her in the direction of the cockpit, and as she edged along beside the pilothouse, he remained to do something with the bowline and the moment was lost.

The tender was secured, both ice chests were loaded in the car, and Dotty had taken her books and her happy memories and headed home to Wanchese. Kiel and Willy were cutting across the parking lot to the Porsche when someone hailed them.

"Kiel! Kielly, where have you been?"

They both halted abruptly as a tiny doll-like creature

detached herself from the side of the silver-gray vehicle and skipped across the marled lot to throw her arms around Kiel's neck. At least, she reached up toward his neck, but even with three-inch heels, she was only able to reach the collar of his shirt and she grabbed it and hung on while she chided him in a clear, ringing drawl that could be heard all over the marina.

"Oh, Kielly, darlin', I thought you'd never get back! I've been waitin' here for ever so long, and . . ."

The voice went on and on and Willy stood back and watched in exasperated amusement. Kielly, darlin', didn't seem to be too happy about seeing her, whoever she was, for he was busy trying to disengage himself, in spite of the fact that the girl was a pint-sized knockout, with magnolia skin, a waving mop of blue-black hair and eyes the color of a blue-enameled Easter egg Willy had had as a child.

"Melanie, what on earth are you doing here? I thought you were going to stay put until you heard from me," Kiel sighed.

"But, Kielly, I wasn't having any fun at all, and you didn't call or write and Atlanta is just so hot in the summertime, and— Well, I thought I'd just come on along and help you out. Aren't you glad to see me?" That last was added on with a delectable pout and Willy made some noise in spite of herself, for they both looked around at the same time.

"Who's this?" the girl sniffed.

"Melanie, this is Wilhelmina Silverthorne. Willy, Melanie Fredericks."

The backseat of the 928S wasn't made for legs as long as Willy's and she bit back her impatience as she watched five feet, nothing curl up in the front seat and anoint Kiel with a look that was pure syrup. Her own look was less than sweet as she tried to keep her chin from bumping against her knees.

Over the purr of the powerful 4664-cc engine she could hear Melanie's plaintive little-girl voice telling Kiel how she had prevailed on her father to fly her to Manteo. "And then I had to hire a man to drive me when I couldn't find you. Your secretary said she thought you might be sailing this weekend and so I came to see if the *Tern* was here and I've been waiting ever since."

"Any reason you decided to come, other than the fact that you weren't having any fun and Atlanta was hot?" Kiel asked dryly as he turned off Highway 12 near South Nags Head.

"I missed you," she said coyly, and Willy had a ringside view of fanning lashes that were long and thick enough to create a draft. Of course, her own were equally long and thick; only, when they were blond, it didn't seem to count.

In the rearview mirror, Kiel's eyes caught Willy's for a brief moment, but when he spoke, it was to the girl beside him. "You could have called. Where are you staying?"

"Why, with you, darlin'," came the immediate rejoinder.

"I'm afraid that won't be very practical."

"But, darlin', when have I ever been practical?" She cast a glance over her shoulder to where Willy sat, contorted around her flight bag and the two ice chests and said disarmingly, "Isn't that just like a man? They want a woman to be all soft and feminine and helpless, and then, all of a sudden, when it suits them, she has to be practical as well." Then, with a surprisingly calculating look in her limpid eyes, "Where do we drop you,

Miss . . . oh, dear, I'm afraid I never was very good with names."

"We don't drop Miss Silverthorne anywhere, Melanie. She was my guest aboard the *Good Tern* this weekend and she lives next door to my own place. Now, where do we drop *you?*" The iron in his voice was unmistakable and evidently it even managed to get through that thick mop of blue-black waves.

"Well, you don't have to bite my head off, Kiel Faulkner. How was I to know Miss Silverthing was a special friend of yours? She doesn't look like your usual type, and anyway, I thought you were supposed to be busy finding out all about this—"

"We'll talk later, Melanie," Kiel interrupted curtly. "Now, if you don't have a place to stay lined up, you'd better come in with me and we'll do some calling around."

It was on the tip of Willy's tongue to offer a couch, but somehow, she didn't think Miss Georgia Peach would appreciate her humble lodgings.

They reached Wimble Court in hot, uncomfortable silence and Willy remained a captive while Kiel wrenched himself out from under the wheel and slammed the door. He strode around the low, sleek hood and jerked open the door, staring grimly off into space as Melanie shimmied her pink-clad body out onto the pavement beside him. One of her plump little alabaster arms worked its way up his chest and her fingers teased his sideburn. "Don't be cross with me, Kielly, darlin' . . . it's been such a tiresome day and I had to wait for hours in that smelly ol' place while you were out there having a good time without me."

Impatiently, Kiel moved her aside and folded back the seat to allow Willy to get out. She would have ignored his hand if it had been at all possible, but she needed help in levering herself out of the confined space, and when she emerged, slightly off balance, she found herself too close for comfort, especially as every move they made was being closely observed by a pair of enameled blue eyes.

"Thanks. It's been fun," Willy said coolly. "I know Dotty enjoyed it, too, in case she got off in too big a hurry to tell you."

"Oh, then you two weren't alone?" Melanie put in brightly.

Willy forestalled whatever it was that Kiel opened his mouth to say by telling the younger girl that there had been three of them and they met others at Hatteras by prearrangement. She could almost see the feathers settling nicely back in place again when Kiel, with malice aforethought, said softly, "But it was nice of you to see that I didn't get lonely while Dotty was studying, and the night she spent aboard the *Eldorado*."

God, what a silly, childish bunch of idiots! All this innuendo and jealousy, as if there were anything between Kiel and herself to threaten someone like Melanie. Her attachment must be secure and of long standing to give her the brassbound gall to turn up on his doorstep with the ingenuous little statement that "It was hot in Atlanta!"

Willy turned and stalked away, and when she reached the foot of her stairway, Kiel stopped her with the reminder that her car was in his garage, and then there was *that* bit to rectify and explain to a newly suspicious Melanie. By the time she got upstairs to her own apartment, she was thoroughly put out. She had closed the place up against a possible rain and it was stuffy, and Melanie, with her pink and white prettiness and her possessive attitude toward Kiel, irritated her; besides, she was hungry!

Having dumped her flight bag unceremoniously on the bed, she was prodding the uninspired contents of her refrigerator when the phone rang. Thinking it was Kiel, with another chapter and verse about his little friend, she let it ring, but then she decided if she didn't answer it, he'd only come over and barge in on her.

It was Matt Rumark. He wanted to know if she and Dotty had had a good weekend and how long they had been back and would she be interested in going to a beach party.

With an excuse already on the tip of her tongue, she heard herself agreeing. Feeling oddly restless and out of sorts, she decided a big, noisy, brash party was exactly what she needed to wipe away the taste of the weekend and its aftermath, and what's more, she decided to have a whale of a good time! Let those two untangle their own affairs; her own feelings were turbulent enough without worrying about what went on between Kiel and Little Miss Cotton Candy!

There had been very few people in Willy's life who had had an immediate adverse effect on her. Her father's third and present wife had been one, and Randy's secretary, Claudia Dunn, had been another. Not that there had ever been more than a few words exchanged between the two of them, for Claudia had had her heart set on being more than a secretary to the head of CCE; and when he had begun to show more than a passing interest in a freckled bean pole who, as often as not, was barefoot, bare-faced and dressed with about as much style as your average scarecrow, it had been too much for someone of Claudia's fastidious nature. She had indicated her dislike of Willy by

112

freezingly contemptuous looks whenever the two of them had come in contact at work, and it had amused as well as irritated Willy to see a woman who dressed as if she were on her way to a fashion show and even in the most melting weather looked bandbox fresh at the end of the day.

So now she could add someone else to her list of least-favorite people. Melanie Fredericks. And there wasn't a single logical reason for that instinctive antipathy except for one she found unacceptable.

Jealousy was a demeaning emotion and she turned her mind determinedly to the evening ahead of her as she fastened on a pair of tortoiseshell ear hoops. She selected a dress she knew was a favorite of Matt's, a red and gold cotton print with an elasticized band under the bust and a low, elasticized scoop neckline that made the most of her long neck and nicely sloped shoulders, and she focused her attention on getting herself into a party mood.

When she heard Matt's tap on her screened door, she sang out, "Come on in. Be ready in a minute," and located her straw sandals and matching bag, noticing impatiently that the clasp would not stay closed.

She looked at her neckline again and sighed, tugging it to cover the half-bra she wore. A little cleavage never hurt anyone and she was certainly used to running around in a lot less than this, on the beach, at least, but lately she had been growing more and more self-conscious about her body.

Just then the door to her bedroom was pushed open from its half-closed position and there, staring at her from the shadowy hallway, was the man who was responsible for that self-consciousness.

"I thought you were Matt."

"I could have been any tramp off the highway, for all you knew," Kiel said sternly. "Willy, you've got to wise up. I don't like to think of you here by yourself with the place wide open like this."

"Then don't. I'm no concern of yours," she retorted.

"Dammit, we're friends, but even if we were strangers. I'd— Here, let me do that." He had crossed the floor with impatient strides and now he took the straw bag she had been fumbling with into his own hands. "It's worn out," he said curtly after half a minute. "Buy yourself a new one," and he tossed it on her bed.

Willy straightened to her full five feet, eight, angry at him for barging in on her in this high-handed way and angry at herself for allowing him to affect her. "Don't tell me what to do, Kiel Faulkner! And furthermore, get out of my bedroom! Get out of my house, in fact!"

"I'll get out when I'm damned good and ready and not before!"

"What did you come up here for, anyway?" she demanded crossly, her eyes riveted to the pulse that hammered just above the pelt of body hair that showed above his open shirt.

"I came to apologize!" he barked. And then, as his eyes crinkled in sardonic amusement, "I came to apologize, Willy. Melanie can be pretty tactless sometimes and she has the manners of a delinquent brat, and so before you're subjected to any more of her thoughtlessness, I wanted to explain a few things about our relationship."

"You've no need to explain a thing, Kiel, and certainly no need to apologize. Just because you invited me along on a sailing weekend is no reason why I should horn in on your old friendships, for goodness' sake."

"Oh, hell, Willy, it's more than that and you know it. All right, Melanie *is* an old friend. Our families have been close for generations and there's nothing they want more than to see the two families joined."

A cold hand closed around Willy's heart and she tried to attach a smile to her face, but it wouldn't stay put. Kiel had turned away and now he stood staring broodingly down at the broken concrete pad between the two houses. "Then where's the problem?" she heard herself say in a voice that was remarkably calm under the circumstances.

"The problem is that something came up and the engagement was broken and I thought I could do a repair job on it, but it looks as if I'm the *last* one to get involved." He shot her an anguished look. "It's a long story, Willy, and you need to hear it from start to finish, but I don't want to get into it if you're expecting Rumark." He looked his question at her and she nodded her head.

"Matt's taking me to a party, a beach party. I'm expecting him momentarily." She wanted him to get out, to leave before her composure shattered and she made a big fool of herself.

"Tomorrow night, then?"

"I don't think so, Kiel. Melanie's sure to have plans for the two of you and, besides, what's between the two of you doesn't concern me at all."

"Damn you, it *does* concern you! That's just the trouble, it concerns you more than anyone else!" He had clamped his hands on her shoulders and now he shook her roughly. "Why won't you let me see you tomorrow night?" he demanded.

"Because I don't want to! There, are you satisfied?"

"No, damn you, I'm not satisfied! Whether you want

to or not, you're going to listen to me!" he asserted, his hands biting into the tender area between her neck and her shoulder joint.

"You're hurting me!" she cried, trying to wrench herself away. "Hadn't you better hurry back? Your little girlfriend's over there with nothing to do except practice her simper and she may get bored."

A gleam of pure malicious amusement lit those obsidian eyes and he eased his grip to allow his hands to slide down her arms. "I called you a cat . . . I wasn't far off the mark, was I? Does it bother you, Willy, that Melanie's over there waiting for me to come back and show her where she's to sleep tonight?"

"Hell, no, it doesn't bother me! As if there were ever any doubt about where she was to sleep! I've heard sailors have one in every port, but maybe you're trying for some kind of a record!" she said acidulously.

"You have no idea what it is I'm trying for, Willy Silverthorne, but this might give you some idea." Allowing her no room to escape, he captured her head with one strong hand and forced her mouth to his. At first she was determined to resist, determined to hold out against that overpowering, undermining attraction that had turned her life upside down, but as he continued to move his lips over hers with soft, sinuous motions, molding her body to him so that she was left in no doubt of the effect she had on him, she gave in.

With a muffled sound that was somewhere between a laugh and a cry, she opened her mouth to him, experiencing again that familiar sharp-sweet reaction that drained the strength from her very bones. Her hands ran up his sides, feeling the lean, taut muscles that covered his ribs and burgeoned into fullness up under his arms and they tucked around behind his shoulders as she curved her body to accommodate him. His own hands were kneading the flesh of her back, and when they moved around to cup the fullness of her breasts, she began to shake her head negatively and pull away from him.

"No, Kiel . . . please, you mustn't," she pleaded, totally unaware that she was still clinging to his shoulders.

He eased the elasticized neckline of her dress down, baring the top of her breasts to his burning gaze and his hands first, then his lips, followed the path of his eyes. When she felt his tongue on the swollen peak of her breast, she panicked, throwing out a barrier she instinctively knew would hold him away.

"Matt . . . Matt will be here any minute. Please, Kiel, you mustn't do this."

"Willy, Willy, forget Rumark. Send him away and let me stay with you tonight." His voice was rough, his hands urgent, and it was all Willy could do not to yield to him, to allow her body the release it cried out for, but she cradled his face in her hands and raised it from her throat, stepping back as she did so that his hands fell away from her sides.

He loomed over her, his eyes burning through her like coals, but he made no effort to touch her again. In the silent room their breath echoed raggedly and it was Willy who regained control of herself first. "You're forgetting Melanie, Kiel," she reminded him, wishing she could forget as easily as he seemed able to do.

"Melanie, hell! Do you think she matters to me now, tonight? Just because Melanie was—and will be again, I hope—engaged to my half-brother is no reason why—"

"Your half-brother!" Willy exclaimed.

He looked at her curiously. "I told you. Didn't I?

117

Good Lord, you don't think Melanie and I . . .?" He laughed incredulously. "But then, why would I be trying so damned hard to—"

"To get me to bed?" she finished for him, perversely angry for all the agony she had felt in one or two short moments. "Why not? I haven't noticed too many scruples where men are concerned."

"Scruples! And women abound in them, I suppose! What the hell do you think brought me down here in the first place? It's not as if I didn't have my own business to tend to, as well as other interests to fill my spare time! Let me tell you something about scruples, lady—"

"And don't call me lady! The only time a man calls a woman a lady is when he's damned certain she's not! Melanie may tell you she's interested in patching up whatever mess she got herself into with your brother, but let me tell you something, Kiel Faulkner, that girl's no more interested in your brother than—than I am!"

"And that's the irony of all times," he said bitterly.

Outside, a car door slammed, shattering the brittle tension that stretched between them like glittering ice. "Why don't you get the hell out of my house, Kiel?" she said with soft intensity. "In fact, why don't you get the hell out of my life?"

He stared at her wordlessly as the sound of footsteps neared the upstairs door, and then he turned and left, brushing the door to her bedroom impatiently so that it clattered hollowly against the Sheetrock walls.

With one hand resting on her stomach as if she could stay the fierce pain that shot through her body, she braced herself to greet Matt as if her world hadn't collapsed around her head. How could she have allowed herself to get in such a state? She loved the man!

Oh, Lord, yes, she loved him until she thought she might die of it, and so she yelled at him like a fishwife and sent him straight back into the comforting arms of a conniving little creature like Melanie Fredericks.

Engaged to his brother! Willy was woman enough to recognize what went on in that pretty little head, and it was not sisterly affection that had brought Miss Fredericks hotfooting it up to North Carolina. Men could be such fools about those things, but Willy was in no position to call anyone else a fool. Hadn't she made the greatest fool of all time of herself, after vowing to play the game by her own rules from now on, rules that didn't permit her to lose?

What she hadn't allowed for was a renegade player who would break every rule in the book and get away with the whole pot, which, in this case, just happened to be her heart!

Chapter Seven

The party was a doubtful success. The location was great: a private beach belonging to one of the fortunate property owners who retained riparian rights. And the crowd was lively and attractive enough. There were melons and barbecued fish, steamed clams and marinated shrimp, and of course, plenty of beer and wine to wash it all down. The moon was a golden sovereign, scattering its gleaming largess across a restless black sea, and a trio of string musicians managed to stay reasonably in tune in spite of the humidity.

Matt was in a strange mood. He seemed almost determined to have a good time, and Willy, who had begun the evening in the same frame of mind, became increasingly aware of the brooding look that crept over his nice-looking features whenever he forgot to keep a smile in place.

It was not Matt's mood, however, that prevented Willy from enjoying herself as she normally would have. It was the knowledge she had faced after Kiel had stormed out earlier, the knowledge that she had gone far beyond a mere surface attraction, that she had made the fatal mistake of falling flat on her face in love with the man, in spite of all her resolutions, her common sense and her past experiences. The laughable thing was that Kiel Faulkner was wealthy enough in his own right not to be influenced by her father's bankroll, even if he had known about it.

It was not his wealth, though, that made Willy, like every woman he came into contact with, look at him with naked longing. He stood head and shoulders above any man she had ever met, in all ways, and she knew instinctively that no matter how physically attracted she was to any man, she could never love him unless she respected him as a person.

For the hundredth time tonight, she dragged her thoughts away from that fruitless subject and set herself out to cheer Matt up. The party centered about the deck and boardwalk that ran from the Cramers' cottage out to the ocean side of the dunes, and Willy peeled off her sandals and jumped lightly to the sand. "Come on, Matthew, don't be an old stodge! Go wading with me!"

"Stodge, am I? You'll regret those words, Wilhelmina Silverthorne," he promised, finishing off his drink and then removing his shoes and socks. He rolled up the legs of his light blue slacks and unbuttoned his shirt with a burlesqued leer in her direction, and perhaps for the first time that night, Willy laughed wholeheartedly. "How're you going to roll up your dress?" he taunted, taking two cold beers from the cooler and jumping down on the hard-packed sand beside her.

"Ahhhh, I has me ways," she teased, skipping on ahead of him. "Give me your belt."

"Good Lord, woman, can't you even wait until we're alone?"

Willy was amused, if slightly surprised. Any other man could have made such a remark and she would have never given it a second thought, but Matt—conservative, serious, straitlaced Matthew—didn't usually deal in innuendo, even as a joke.

She swooped up the long skirt of her dress and brought it up between her legs, holding it at the waistline like an enormous pair of baggy bloomers. "*Voilà!* Instant waders," she cried, and he took off his belt and handed it to her. Luckily, it was a stretchable one and they both laughed as she wrapped it around her twice and still managed to buckle it . . . just.

For several minutes, they walked silently, allowing the damp, pungent atmosphere to envelop them in its own exotic ambience, but when Willy felt Matt's gloom slipping back over him, she asked for one of the beers he carried, in spite of the fact that she had never cultivated a taste for the stuff. For a few minutes, that served as a topic of conversation and they discussed various beers, imported and domestic, but gradually the silence overtook them again. This time she tried to awaken his interest by kicking up the wet sand to reveal the bits of phosphorus that gleamed among the grains, but he only grunted and plodded along, hands in his pockets.

With a desperate sort of gaiety, as much for her own sake as for his, Willy sang out, "I don't know about you, but I'm in the mood for a swim!" She spun away, running lightly down the beach away from the colorful light of the lanterns, and she could hear Matt's feet pounding along after her as he called out sternly that swimming at night was dangerous.

It spurred her on, although she had no intention of going in swimming. With the damp, warm wind combing through her hair and only the vague, phosphorescent gleam of the surf ahead of her, it was almost as if she could outrun the heartache she had brought with her tonight, until all at once a sharp pain stabbed through her left foot and she doubled over and sunk to the ground with a small cry.

Matt was beside her almost instantly, bending over with concerned murmurings as she swayed back and forth. "Did you twist it?" he asked, dropping to his knees beside her.

"No," she managed through clenched teeth, "I think I stepped on something—a shell, probably. It's wet, Matt. Do you have a handkerchief?" She knew the skin was broken, but more than that she couldn't tell here in the dark. She had once had a tiny shell cut that had hurt like the very devil and that was probably all it was . . . nothing to make a big fuss over. All the same, she took Matt's handkerchief and tied it awkwardly about her heel, standing up with only the slightest of gasps. "I think I've about had it for tonight," she told him as they turned to retrace their steps along the beach.

Janette Cramer was all sympathy and wanted to take Willy to the cottage and render first aid, but Willy managed to convince her that it was only a scratch and that she'd look after it at home, and they left, with Matt all concerned support. She tried not to hobble, but to tell the truth, it was throbbing worse by the minute.

Matt drove fast, faster than he might have had he not consumed several beers earlier, but she couldn't be concerned with that now. Her own head was feeling the effects of a too-long, too-eventful day, plus the several glasses of wine she had imbibed. Impossible to believe that only this morning she had been lolling about on a ketch off Hatteras. Tonight's party had been a mistake, for more reasons than one, she conceded tiredly.

"Willy, I wouldn't have had this happen for the world, especially not now," Matt said, braking for a long line of theater traffic.

"Thanks," she gritted, "but now's as good as any time, I guess. At least I'll have a good excuse to be late tomorrow."

"You don't understand."

"What don't I understand?" she sighed, wishing he'd be quiet.

"Willy, I hate this like the very devil, but I'm going to have to let somebody go. There's not enough work for two, much less for four, and— Well, I wanted to be fair about it, but I just don't see how I can afford to be."

Oddly enough, she was almost relieved—light-headed, for some strange reason. Matt had been carrying the weight of the world on his poor, sweet shoulders all night, and come to find out, it had only been this. "Well, of course, you must be fair, darling. I was the last to come and so I'll be the first to go."

"No, Willy, that's just it; you weren't. Pete came in a week after you did, remember?"

And she did. Remembering that, she could see the wretched problem poor Matt had been wrestling with all evening, and who knew how long before that? Certainly since that discouraging little meeting in his office. And now that she thought of it, she was aware of the meaningful little glances, the puzzling looks she had been getting from both Frank and Pete for at least the past week or so.

Then, like a bag of water bursting on her head, she recalled that night at the Drake when Matt had sounded her out about her feelings on raising a family, and on one breadwinner in a family being enough. She had thought he was working his cautious, tedious way around to proposing to her. Lord, was the laugh ever on her! She had been the very last one to see the handwriting on the wall, and now, feeling more than a little illiterate, she said, "I'll take off, Matt. Shall I work out my notice or just clear out my desk?"

They were almost at the corner of Wimble Court and Willy saw that the streetlight was out again, making her glad she had remembered for once to leave on her own stair light. It was after midnight and it would have been as black as pitch, for everyone on the short street turned in early and the fickle moon had either set or gone behind clouds.

Matt parked between the two houses and Willy saw that there was a faint glimmer of light from Kiel's screened porch—the cork-based hurricane lamp, no doubt. She turned woodenly to hear Matt saying, "Look, Willy, I'd rather cut my tongue out for what I'm having to say, but Pete's got Kip and Connie and she's pregnant again and—"

"I know, honey. They're buying a house and paying for a car and I'm just a female, not the head of a household or anything so dramatic." There was resignation in her voice, as well as a reluctant hint of indignation. After all, you'd think women didn't have to eat or pay rent and living expenses, and besides, her foot ached like the very devil and she was beginning to feel just a bit sorry for herself! "Don't worry about it, Matt. I was beginning to get slightly bored, anyway. Things haven't been particularly exciting around there since the novelty wore off."

"It's not as though you'd starve, or anything like that," he said apologetically, and she gathered up her bag and sandals impatiently. "I mean, you can't be hurting all that bad."

"Oh, sure! I'll just pawn the family jewels or sell off a few blocks of stock," she said brightly. "About my notice . . .?" Matthew Rumark, she thought silently, you have no idea how badly I'm hurting right now, in my head, in my foot and in my heart!

"But your father— I mean, he'll look after you . . . get you another job if you want it, surely?"

"My who?" she repeated wonderingly, halted in the act of opening the door with the Rumark Realty logo painted on it in dark green letters. "Matt, what do you know about my father?"

In the dim light of the interior, she turned to look at him with dawning realization, seeing the averted face, the guilt painted all over that thin, straight nose, the light gray eyes and the slightly sloping chin. "Matthew?"

"Hell, Willy, I didn't want you to have to know. Your father won't be any too happy about it, either," he admitted ruefully. It seemed that he had been in indirect contact with her father from the beginning of her employment at Rumark Realty.

"But my letters, Jasper's letters," she faltered indignantly, remembering all the letters her father had sent with the checks that she had promptly torn up. "They were all sent through Cousin Fred."

"Who just happens to be in real estate in Edenton, who also just happens to be the contact that got you the job with me," Matt interposed.

"And you—you've been reporting to my father every time I made a sale, no doubt," she accused belligerently. "Oh, you've no idea how great that makes me feel! Little Willy, making it on her own!"

"No, Willy it wasn't that way at all," Matt exclaimed defensively. "Your father only wanted to know how you were getting on and you weren't very forthcoming in your letters, from what I heard."

"Oh, you had a nice little setup going there, didn't you? Every move I made was duly reported on behind my back!"

"Dammit, Willy, he was interested, that's all! I mean, you *are* his daughter, after all, and he *is* in real estate himself."

"Jasper? You must be kidding!" she crowed bitterly. "When you're in real estate to the extent that my father is, then you're not in real estate at all! You're all the way out the other end!"

She threw open the door and climbed out and almost crumpled to the ground when her injured heel touched the concrete. She had all but forgotten it in the ensuing discussion!

"Let me come help you take care of that, my dear," Matt said, hurrying around to slide an arm under her own.

She tried to push him away, but there was no escaping the fact that she could use help in getting up the stairs, but that was all! When he asked if he could come in and look after her, after managing her lurching ascent, she shook her head. With each step she had felt her anger and indignation drain away, leaving only the bitter dregs of empty disappointment in its place. It wasn't Matt's fault, the relationship she had with Jasper, nor could he have ignored the Silverthorne style of coercion: subtle, smooth and inescapable.

"No, thanks, Matt," she said tiredly. "I can do it up just fine with a tad of iodine and a Band Aid. All in all, it's been quite a party." She tried for a smile, failed miserably and gave up, closing the screened door after him and leaning her head against its damp, acrid-smelling surface. Before she turned away, she saw the dim light on Kiel's porch go off.

Five hours and three aspirin later, Willy thought with painful amusement that had she been in her father's house, there would have been at least one specialist in attendance, plus a stiffly starched nurse. She had never been allowed even to scrape her knee without its being made into a major production. Funny, she thought without much amusement, her father had never hid his disappointment that she had turned out to be a girl—and a not very attractive girl at that—at least not until she was too old for his disappointment to hurt very badly. Still, he had lavished on her every care money could buy, as long as it didn't require his personal attention. She didn't want to have to return ignominiously now, to see his good-looking, whiskey-flushed features assume that Father-knows-best expression. He might welcome her with compunction, but Breda would be less than hospitable.

No, darn it, she had bought her independence dearly, even if he had been aware of every step she had taken, and she wouldn't go back to that suffocating silken cocoon and wait around for him to buy her a suitable husband! Just because the real world held a few rude awakenings was no reason to turn tail and go crying back to Daddy!

For some odd reason of association, she thought of a sugary drawl telling Kiel how Daddy had flown her to Manteo. It seemed that all in the world Daddy Fredericks wanted was for his little girl to be happy: maybe daddies had that in common.

With a rude noise, she swung her feet off the bed and

just as quickly swung them back again. It felt as if a ton of bricks had dropped on her heel, and now she twisted her injured foot up into a half-lotus position and frowned at the angry red puffiness around the thin, dark red line. She had soaked it in hot water and applied an antiseptic before she went to bed, but it looked as if stronger measures were called for.

There was no question of her driving to work, and so perhaps it was just as well she didn't feel any great compunction about clearing out her desk. It would be awkward at best for poor Pete, knowing that by all rights he should be the one to go—unless Matt had told them all about her background, in which case they were probably furious with her for taking a job away from some worthy breadwinner. Oh, drat! All she needed now to complete the picture was a load of guilt!

All she needed now was help, she corrected herself. She looked in the direction of Kiel's house and knew she could never ask him to take her to see a doctor, and Ada Willits would be asleep with her earplugs after having just got home from the nightshift at the convenience store.

Dotty. She needed help right now and Dotty was the one to supply it with a minimum of fuss. She hopped across the gritty linoleum and dialed the Wanchese number, hoping she wasn't too late. While the receiver buzzed in her ear, she strained to see the alarm clock, but it wasn't running and Willy despised to wear a watch, especially as her one and only timepiece was a bracelet affair with more diamonds than good taste required.

"Hello, Dotty? It's me, Willy. Look, are you running late this morning?"

It turned out that Dotty wasn't and that she would be glad to stop by on her way to work, since it was practically on her way.

Just what Willy expected of her, she wasn't sure herself, but somewhere in the back of her mind was the ingrained feeling that at a time like this, someone else would just automatically step in and take over, making all decisions and arrangements. It had always happened that way in the past, but then this was the present. So far, she had been lucky, never having had anything more serious than a headache or an occasional touch of indigestion from some of her less successful experiments in the kitchen.

"Ugh, that looks dreadful, Willy," was Dotty's comforting exclamation on being shown the wounded appendage. "Have you seen a doctor?"

"Well, of course not! It just happened last night— well, this morning, actually. Matt called after we got in yesterday and we went to a beach party at Southern Shores."

"Last night?" Dotty squawked. "I was flaked out by the time I got home! In fact, I wasn't even sure I was going to make it all the way home. Being on the water always affects me that way, makes me drowsy as everything and I rock for days with my eyes closed."

"Sounds cozy," Willy agreed sourly, wriggling her toes in an effort to get a better look at the sole of her foot. "I wish I'd had the good sense to stay home where I belonged. Who's a good doctor in these parts?"

Dotty named her own physician and offered to call, and Willy let her, wondering if she'd be able to drive. It was her left foot and she might have managed with an automatic transmission, supposing she didn't need to brake, but with a clutch, it was out of the question. Still, she'd have to think of something.

"Look, don't even try to come to work today," Dotty warned her, a frown giving her an unexpectedly mature look.

Oh, yes, there was that too. Evidently Matt had not informed the rest of the staff of his plans to sack the most affluent member of the sales force. "Well, as a matter of fact, with things so slow around there, I thought I might try my hand at something else for a change. I mean, there's no law that says I have to stick with my first job. I told Matt last night I probably wouldn't be in today, under the circumstances." She felt noble and martyred and sorry for herself, and then, hard on the heels of all those demeaning emotions, came a refreshing feeling of self-disgust.

Here she was, young, unattached, healthy—well, relatively, anyway—and with enough security behind her to buy and sell Rumark Realty and all its assets, and she had the nerve to feel sorry for herself! The only thing she lacked was the one thing in the world she really wanted, but she wasn't going to go breaking her badly bruised heart just because one arrogant, amoral, all too attractive man wanted to have his cake and eat it too!

Dotty hung up the phone with the information that the doctor could see her at two-thirty today and, meanwhile, she was to keep her foot up and uncovered.

Well, that ought to be easy enough to do, seeing as how she didn't feel like doing anything else, though getting to the doctor's office was another matter—but it seemed she had reckoned without Dotty.

"Look, I know you can't drive with that thing

looking like a pink satin pincushion, so I'm going to come by at two and help you get dressed and drive you to see the doctor, all right?"

With no choice, Willy was forced to agree. She said good-bye and promised to look after herself, and then wondered why, with all her problems solved so neatly, she still felt tears rising in her throat.

It was Dotty, she supposed. Until she had come to work at Rumark Realty, she had never had a close friend—hardly a friend at all, only suitable acquaintances who enjoyed suitable pastimes, all of which bored Willy stiff.

By one o'clock, Willy was utterly miserable. Her head was pounding and she felt hot and sticky and she was afraid to take a shower. She hobbled to the bathroom and sponged herself off, grimacing when the circulation increased in the leg she had kept elevated all morning.

At one-thirty she pulled off her cool, cotton hip-length pajamas and tugged on a denim skirt and a flowered T-shirt. Her hair was brushed halfheartedly and pulled back with a scarf that didn't match anything she was wearing, and she located a pair of rubber flip-flops and slid her feet in them. Not a very fashionable turnout, but then, this was hardly a festive occasion—not that she did a whole lot better when it *was* a festive occasion, she thought with wry self-deprecation.

At a quarter of two, the door opened and Kiel Faulkner walked in.

"Hi," she greeted, having conveniently forgotten the last time she had seen him, when she told him rudely to get the hell out of her house and out of her life. "Did you need anything?"

He dropped down onto her only comfortable chair, looking unfairly cool and unflappable in white jeans and a dark green shirt. "Do you see a measuring cup?" he asked sardonically. "Do I have to have a reason to drop in on a friend?"

"No, but . . ." Nothing to do but barge ahead; Willy was not one to indulge in equivocation. "But after the last time we parted I didn't think I'd be seeing you again."

"Last night," he mused. "Well, you were pretty outspoken with your advice for my future behavior, if I recall correctly, but then I'm here today as a favor to Dotty. She and I haven't had a falling out and so I have no reason to refuse to help her out of a tight spot, have I?"

Pushing back an unruly tendril of hair that had already pulled loose from the scarf, she eyed him suspiciously. This bland urbanity was even more unsettling than his outspoken anger.

"No arguments? Good. If you're ready, then, we'll be off. Dotty said the doctor was going to try and work you in about two-thirty, but if we get there a little earlier, he may be able to see you sooner."

"Hey, wait a minute! Dotty's going to take me there," Willy protested.

Kiel explained with exaggerated patience that Dotty, as the one and only secretary at Rumark Realty, was far more indispensable than one engineer in a room full of engineers.

"Somehow, I don't think it works out quite that way over at CCE," Willy gritted, trying to work up her nerve to lower her foot to the floor again. "How did you know about it, anyway?"

He leaned over and scooped her up before she could get her balance, and when she started to argue, he simply tightened his grip in a meaningful way until she subsided. "When the men started getting restless wondering what had happened to you—your public, you know—I called over and asked. Dotty was a mine of information, and so I repaid her by offering to take you off her hands this afternoon."

He flipped the latch on her door to lock it behind him and descended the stairs easily.

Funny, how you could distrust a man with your heart and still trust him with your very life, Willy mused wistfully as he tucked her solicitously into the front seat.

Judging from the way they were greeted, you'd think the doctor had been waiting impatiently for their arrival. It just so happened that he could see her immediately, and she insisted on hobbling into his inner sanctum alone, leaving Kiel to pass his time leafing through back issues of *North Carolina Wildlife* and *Woman's Day*.

By the time she emerged, soaked, swabbed, bandaged and injected, she was too drained to complain when he swept her up in his arms again. She even managed a wicked grin at the offended woman with the sensible shoes and the flowered hat.

Shouldering his way outside into the broiling sun, he paused and studied her with one eyebrow elevated expressively. "I know just what you need to put you back into fighting trim again."

Several minutes later she was ensconced at a picnic table in the shade of an enormous live oak while Kiel disappeared into the ice-cream parlor nearby. He emerged just as she was beginning to think he had deserted her with a pair of the gaudiest concoctions she had seen since her seventh birthday.

"Good Lord, do you eat 'em or wear 'em," she gurgled, forgetting her throbbing foot for the moment.

"If you don't eat it immediately, you'll be wearing it right enough," he warned, handing over one of the plastic bowls filled with three colors of ice cream, whipped cream, crushed pineapple, chocolate syrup and a topping of crystallized ginger, "because the damned things are highly perishable."

She took him at his word, tackling it suspiciously from the side. "I see now why you insisted on getting me out of the car."

"You're catching on fast . . . watch that drip on the side! Now, aren't you glad Dotty rang in a substitute? She'd never have thought of this."

"Ice cream to make it all better?" Willy murmured, slanting him a playful look as she caught a sliding mound of whipped cream.

"Just one among several traditional folk cures," he returned.

"Yes, well, this one happens to be a favorite of mine."

They concentrated on eating for the next few minutes, and when they were finished, Kiel took both bowls and went off in search of a place to wet his handkerchief. Napkins wouldn't suffice. He was back shortly, and by then, Willy had steeled herself against his insidious charm. She took the wet handkerchief and wiped her mouth and hands and then asked idly, "Where's Melanie today?"

"Claudia offered to take her in tow and show her the

sights. They mentioned the Elizabethan Gardens and Fort Raleigh and maybe the Marine Resources Center if there was time, but I have an idea they won't get beyond the biggest emporium on the beach."

"You'll have to show her around later. After all, she didn't come all this way to be fobbed off with your secretary."

"No, as a matter of fact, she came all this way to see if I had made any progress in finding out about the woman who broke up her engagement to my half-brother."

Willy twisted to ease her foot. "Is that what you came down here for? I thought you were here to take Randy Collier's place at CCE? You mean your brother's—well, whatever she was—is in this area, too?" Thoroughly confused, Willy frowned at him, wishing she had brought along her dark glasses against the brilliant sun. Kiel's face was totally unreadable, silhouetted as it was against the afternoon sky.

He stood up immediately. "Come on, let's go home. This is no place to talk. Besides, the doctor said something about starting on antibiotics immediately, didn't he? Well, let's go get you taken care of and then we have a few things to sort out."

To tell the truth, Willy was more than ready to leave. The infection that had flared so quickly had had a systemic effect on her and some of the exhilaration she had felt on first seeing Kiel had worn off now, leaving her hot and tired and achy.

There was no more talk on the way home. During the ten-minute ride Kiel concentrated on driving in a way that didn't jar her foot and he insisted on carrying her up her stairs when they reached Wimble Court. "I saw you when you got home last night," he told her as he managed the key without even shifting his burden. "I don't mind telling you I thought about coming over and letting you in on a few home truths. I was still mad as hell, but when I saw Rumark helping you up the stairs, it looked to me as if you were both about three sheets to the wind." He grinned down at her in the doorway. "If it's any comfort to you, I didn't sleep worth a damn!"

Willy laughed and ducked her head. "If it's any comfort to you, I didn't, either," she admitted.

Chapter Eight

Just for an instant when Kiel lowered her onto the sofa, Willy caught an objective glimpse of the room that had come to be home to her in the past few months. Shiny varnish on paneled walls, a ceiling that was marked from the frequent hard rains and an assortment of furniture that only a mother could love; all the same, it would be a wrench to have to leave it. She leaned back her head and closed her eyes and she heard Kiel sliding open the door that let out onto her upstairs porch. Unlike his, hers was not screened, but it didn't seem to matter too much. There was usually a breeze off the ocean and mosquitoes didn't fly above forty feet, her landlord had told her optimistically.

She opened her eyes to see Kiel's face with a shaft of sunlight throwing into relief the prominent cheekbones and casting a beam behind the irises of his eyes so that she saw for the first time that they were really a clear, deep gray, not the opaque metallic shade she had supposed.

He sat on the foot of the sofa, taking care not to jar her foot. "I'll get you some water to take your pills with in a minute. First, before we get interrupted by the phone or by Dotty or an itinerant encyclopedia salesman, I want to talk to you."

"I don't know if that's such a good idea," she stalled.

Now that the revelation—whatever it was—was about to become a reality, she was getting cold feet. When someone said they needed to talk to you, it was usually about something you'd just as soon not hear.

"You're probably right," he conceded. "I could use a pot of strong black coffee and you—" He broke off and examined her face with disconcerting thoroughness. "Did you know your eyes were the color of malachite? And there are shadows under them big enough to swallow them? You must have had a hell of a night."

"It wasn't one of my better times," she admitted offhandedly. He was cradling her foot on his lap now, his hand playing idly up and down her shin, and she found it almost impossible to listen to his words when her body was growing increasingly aware of his.

"You really deal yourself a losing hand now and then, don't you?" he asked.

"Who's dealing?" She shrugged. "I stepped on a shell, that's all."

"And got your cut infected and resigned your job. Anything else to add to the list of woes?" His crooked grin with the one chipped tooth in a perfect lineup had the strange effect of irritating her. Or maybe she was only gathering up her defenses.

But before she could arrange them in an impregnable barrier, he had leaned over and gathered her up in his lap, and under the sensuous impact of his direct gaze, she melted, throbbing foot, aching head and all.

"How the hell am I supposed to talk to you when you sit there with your hair falling around your head, your lipstick all eaten off, chocolate on your shirt and a bandaged foot, and all I can think of is how I'm going to manage to get you in my bed?"

With a jolt like the slamming of a door, she felt the dangerous electricity flow through her at his words, that stunning, intoxicating feeling that rendered her all but helpless before his blatant virility. "Don't start that again," she warned shakily, leaning back to escape the full charge from his lambent eyes.

"Too late." He laughed softly against her lips. "It's already started."

And it had. With a fatalistic helplessness, she allowed her arms to move around his shoulders to where she could tangle her fingers in his hair, holding his head above hers while his mouth sought affirmation of what his hands on her breasts were telling him.

Oh, Lord, he didn't know what a losing hand was, she thought wildly as he slid his hands under her shirt to release the catch at her back. Here it was three o'clock of a sultry afternoon, and she was hurting and hungry in spite of the ice cream and all she could think of was what his hands were doing to her, and his mouth . . . and what she'd like for him to be doing to her.

A losing hand, oh, yes, and she had been playing for the highest of stakes, but she gave up and her last rational thought was that she may as well go out in style, as she allowed her own hands to unbutton the front of his shirt and steal their way inside to caress the hard, warm skin beneath.

"Do you know what you're doing to me?" he whispered against her mouth.

She had no answer except to open herself to his kiss, allowing him the full freedom of her lips, his hands the freedom of her body. He caught the weight of her breasts in his hands and held them as if he were holding an unfledged baby bird, and she could have wept at his tenderness, for she had an idea that what force and aggressiveness had failed to accomplish, this destroying gentleness would.

There was scarcely room on the sofa for the two of them and so his body had come to rest partly on hers, and even with his heart pounding in his breast like a captured thing, his breath coming harsh and ragged from tortured lungs, he was infinitely careful not to jar her injured foot. His hand stroked down from her breast to her waist and then slowly rounded her hip and slipped down her thigh, and when it reached her knee, he shifted her leg for greater security and she marveled at his concern for her at a time like this.

"Willy, I can't seem to get much talking done for making love to you and it's important that you understand something," he murmured against her ear when they had kissed each other to the edge of sanity and back again. His hand lay still on her breast and so he was well aware of the condition she was in, nor was his own state any mystery to her. Never had she been so affected by the nearness of any man, and it was far more than his admitted expertise, more than the devastating way the planes and angles of his features fell together. It was simply that she loved him through and through and she was terribly frightened of what it was he had to tell her.

"Does it concern Melanie?" she asked tentatively.

After a brief pause, he said, "Yes, it does."

That was enough. She willed her heart to be still, her eyes to hold her secret, and gathering every vestige of strength left to her, she pushed him away. Not hard . . . that would have required an explanation and she was in no condition to explain anything at the moment, but enough to bring a quick look of concern to his eyes.

"Your foot?" he asked, and she nodded. Better to let

him think that than that it was her heart that was causing her more pain than she could bear. So Melanie was engaged to his brother—his half-brother. Well, Melanie wore no engagement ring, and it was not in a sisterly way that the exquisite young woman looked at him. Just when she reached the point where she didn't think she could hold back a declaration of her own feelings, Melanie's name would enter proceedings and once more she would feel that dreadful fear of rejection all over again. This time she'd take nothing for granted. No man was going to put her in the position Luke Styrewall had done.

"I—I think I'd better take something and try to get some sleep," she told him. "I really didn't get too much last night." Which was no more than the truth, but it wasn't only her foot that had kept her so wakeful in the night. Kiel bore his share of the blame as well.

Carefully, he extracted his long legs from hers and levered his weight up without jarring her. The concern written on his strong features was enough to bring a stinging to her eyes and she turned her face away from him. She could feel him looking down at her, his nearness having an effect on every cell in her body, and then he moved away and she heard him running water into a glass.

"I'll leave a pitcher of iced tea on the coffee table where you can reach it," he told her. "Here, take your pills. Is there anything else I can do to make you more comfortable?"

She was hungry and she wanted something hard and tough to chew, for she felt an overwhelming urge to bite and tear at something that couldn't bite back, but she told him crossly not to fuss over her, just to go, and so he leveled a look at her that made her feel slightly ashamed of herself, and he left.

It had been too hot to sleep. The breeze, even here on the second floor, had dropped to practically nothing and she could hear the steady drone and drip of a window air-conditioner downstairs. Richy's mother, Ada, managed to sleep days only with the air-conditioner, a pair of ear plugs and dark shades at her windows, but her air-conditioner, like most other appliances in the apartment, broke down at least once a month. Maybe she'd be better off finding herself another place to stay, Willy thought irritably as she struggled with a sticking ice tray.

Suddenly the walls seemed to close in on her. Thoughts of her infinitesimal savings, her lack of employment, her father's probable reaction when he learned of her present circumstances, not to mention the mess she had got herself in as far as her foolish heart was concerned, all proved too much to cope with in the uninspiring confines of her shabby room. May as well give the antibiotic something to get its teeth into, she thought grimly, lurching into the bedroom to change into her bikini.

It was a good thing it was too early for Kiel to be back from work. She could imagine what he'd say after her having pleaded invalidism. Dismissing the thought from her mind, she spread her beach towel out on the sand just above the level of the tideline and lowered herself gingerly, taking care to keep her injured foot on the side away from the water. At least if the waves washed over her head, she could hold her bandage up and keep it dry, she thought with a partial return to her normal irreverent sense of humor.

The sun felt marvelous soaking through her skin and the thought of an even greater crop of freckles didn't faze her in the least. She dozed when the soothing susurrus of the surf relaxed her for the first time since yesterday. When she opened her eyes again, instead of the cerulean dome overhead, she looked up into a brass bowl that shaded to copper on the western side. She was actually beginning to feel chilly, believe it or not, and she sat up and considered the easiest way to get to her feet without grinding wet sand into her bandage.

"Hi. I thought I'd come out and join you now that the sun's not so hot. A girl can't be too careful of her complexion, can she? But, of course, you don't have to worry, poor thing."

Twisting her head, she saw Melanie Fredericks drop a velvety towel to the sand beside her and lower herself gracefully.

So much for her precarious peace of mind. Willy settled back into place, bracing herself to think of something pleasant to say when she'd like to have the nerve to ignore the girl and walk away.

"Hello, Melanie. Did you have a good time sightseeing today?"

That brought on a sly, sidelong glance that Willy was in no mood to try and interpret. "Oh, I had an interesting day, all right," drawled the little brunette. "Claudia and I went to her apartment and spent the afternoon talking."

Well, bully for you, Willy thought sourly. She could think of lots more pleasant things to do than to spend an afternoon talking with either of them. Visit the dentist, maybe, or figure her income tax.

"Don't you want to know what we talked about?"

"Not particularly," Willy retorted, turning over on her face and pretending to be sleepy again.

"Oh, you should have been there. You'd have been awfully interested, Willy. What a peculiar name for a girl . . . Willy. Do you like it?"

Irritably, Willy told her that her friends called her Wilhelmina.

"We talked about mutual friends . . . yours, mine and Claudia's," the girl said, pausing expectantly afterward.

Willy rolled over and sat up again. "All right," she sighed, "I can see you're dying to tell me something, so why don't you spit it out!"

"Oh, you *are* crude, aren't you? Claudia said you weren't her sort, and Randy— But of course, Randy would have an entirely different opinion, wouldn't he?"

Inside her, several blocks of ice shifted and settled into a pattern she didn't like, didn't care for at all. "Randy?" she repeated cautiously.

"Randy Collier. You know him?"

"Look, Melanie, you have something on your mind. I'm in no mood to play games, so I suggest you either get to the point or go back inside and leave me in peace. My patience isn't all that good at the moment."

"Well, the point is, Wilhelmina, dear, that you're the woman who broke up my engagement. Now that I see you for myself, I wonder what all the fuss was about. I mean, really, it's not as if you were any big threat or anything. Kiel might just as well not have bothered."

A slow sort of paralysis crept over her mind and she could only stare at the preening little creature in the ice-blue one-piece bathing suit that fit like a second skin, emphasizing the very features it covered. "Kiel might just as well not have bothered with *what?*" she repeated with a sense of dread.

"Well, after all, Randy *is* his half-brother, and when Randy called from Norfolk General and told us he was lying there with a broken leg and all sorts of miserable things, Kiel went rushing off to see him. I mean, what else could he do, especially as we hadn't heard a thing from him in ages." Melanie eyed her expectantly, but Willy was determined not to probe. She waited, dreading what she'd hear next, but when it came, it was worse than anything she could have imagined.

"You see, Randy and I were all set to be married, and then, when we got this letter that said he was making a fool of himself over some greedy little office worker who only went out with men of a certain income level for what she could get out of them, why I was all broken up. I declare, I wept buckets! Simply buckets full, and I told Kielly, and he and Daddy decided he'd better go see what was going on, so," she continued with hardly a pause for air, "Kielly went to the hospital and Randy told him there was this girl who worked at the office next door and she had made a sort of— Well, you know how a girl can do when she's, you know, *in*terested in a man. Well, anyway, poor Randy told her he was engaged and all, but she wouldn't leave him alone and when she threatened to write to his fiancée— that was me," she added ingenuously, "and tell her this whole mess o' lies, well, Randy got all upset and first thing he knew, he was upside down in a ditch."

The air left Willy's lungs in a burst and she closed her eyes. Random impressions whirled dizzyingly in her head and she tried to reach up and catch them and deal with them. How much of what Melanie said was the truth and how much a malicious prank on the part of her and Claudia? Somehow, she couldn't see the older girl playing tricks, no matter how she disliked her, but writing a letter that would damage Willy's position with Randy? Yes, she could easily see her doing something like that.

"Well?" Melanie prompted now, watching her from those perfectly guileless blue eyes.

"Well, what?"

"Don't you have anything to say for yourself?"

Willy moved her shoulders in a gesture of resignation. "What can I say? If you believe that of your fiancé, then you'll be only too glad he escaped my vicious clutches, won't you? When's the wedding?" Randy and Melanie. Now that she knew, it seemed perfect. The trouble was, where did Kiel come into this?

And with that thought, the crux of the matter hit her like a sledgehammer. Kiel had been courting her deliberately! He had set out to meet her. The car, the sherry—had Randy told him how much she enjoyed cooking and about her enthusiasm for good cars? Lord, even that added up to the picture of a mercenary female out for a good time! Something inside her crumpled and she got to her knees and dragged herself up as if she were a hundred years old.

"What's the matter, Willy? Don't tell me you've had enough sunshine?" Melanie taunted softly, stretching herself like a kitten.

Not bothering to answer, Willy scooped up her towel and turned toward the dune, deliberately grinding her cut foot into the sand as if the pain might erase the far worse pain of the past few minutes. She didn't pause when Melanie called after her, but her chin rose a fraction as she continued her escape.

"Just don't get any ideas about the way Kiel's been pretending to be nice to you, honey. He knew all along who you were, he just wanted me to see for myself what sort of a woman you were, one who'd chase any man who looked at her if he had enough money. He doesn't want me to blame poor old Randy, but it really doesn't matter, now. You see, I've already decided to have Kiel instead." She had raised her voice for the last few words, for Willy's progress was more rapid than she might have expected, and the sound of that sugary drawl, sounding slightly shrill as it carried out over the late-afternoon quietness, lingered in Willy's ears for hours, robbing her of an appetite, destroying any chance she might have had for a night's rest.

The phone rang several times, and in desperation, she got dressed and hobbled downstairs to her car. She could handle the clutch and the brakes better than she could any mealymouthed excuses from Kiel Faulkner, she decided grimly as she drove herself toward Oregon Inlet.

With no conscious decision on her part, she found herself in Hatteras. She pulled up into the parking lot at the base of the lighthouse and sat there, her arms resting across the steering wheel, and she realized with a shaky laugh that her chin had been jutting out so far, so long, that her neck muscles were tired. She also made the discovery that she was starving.

An hour and a half later, she sat in her motel room and dialed an outside line. She was replete with a seafood dinner, none of which she even tasted, but at least it had momentarily put an end to that awful hollow feeling inside her. She had been lucky in the matter of a room, coming on a cancellation before any other tired and homeless transient pulled up.

"Hello, Ada? It's me, Willy," she said when the familiar brogue came on the other end.

"Good Lord, Willy, where in the world have you got to? There's been all sorts of bother the past hour or two over you."

Kiel. It could only be Kiel, trying to explain away his behavior, although she hardly saw why he bothered, now that she knew. Certainly he and his little Melanie could pack up and get back to wherever it was they came from—Atlanta, Bar Harbor. "What's wrong, Ada? I'm at Hatteras, and the reason I called, I left—"

"Hatteras!" The exclamation stabbed her ear and she held the receiver away. "Willy, that man across the way's been beatin' my door off the hinges wantin' to know what happened to you, an' I told him plain out I didn't know, because I didn't, but then that other fellow came, and—"

"Matt? Matthew Rumark, my boss?"

"Matthew? No, it was some good-looking dude, older than Matt, but still—you know what I mean—the sort I'd follow if he so much as frowned at me. Drove a fancy car, sort of heavy and foreign-looking and—"

Jasper. It could only be Jasper. "Did he say what he wanted, Ada?" she asked cautiously.

"Nope. Just asked if I knew where you were and when you'd be back, and I told him you was as likely to be out all night as not. Give him something to chew on. Doesn't pay to let 'em think they have you where they want you, not even silver-plated ones like this gent."

She sighed. "Thanks, Ada," she said, hanging up the phone absently. So Jasper had not revealed his relationship to her. He probably thought he was bending over to be fair, allowing her to play at being a poor working girl up to the last minute, she thought bitterly. Well, he could just cool his heels for a spell. She had this room until tomorrow afternoon at least, and she'd just sit tight and work out her next steps before confronting her father. He'd still be there when she finally showed up, making hourly calls or maybe even having the place staked out.

So let him worry a bit. It might arouse some long-dormant paternal streak in him—not that she was at all sure she wanted *that!* She lay in bed staring at the ceiling for a long time, trying to chart a course through a sea of imponderables. She never even thought of the fact that she had forgotten to ask Ada to go up and close her windows if it rained.

And then, with a streak of innate honesty, she admitted to herself that she didn't care if it flooded the whole place; she had only wanted to be told that Kiel had asked after her.

Chapter Nine

Awakening to see the curtains standing straight out from the windows, it occurred to Willy that if her father had been looking for proof that she wasn't capable of looking after herself, she had handed him a platterful. It was blowing a fitful rain from the northeast and she was here without so much as a change of clothes, much less a sweater or a raincoat. For that matter, she probably didn't even have her checkbook with her. What a shiny crowning touch to her career as an independent operator, to have to call on her father to come bail her out.

Deciding there was no point in remaining cooped up here in her motel room until checkout time, she quickly pulled on yesterday's jeans and shirt and did the best she could with neither toothbrush nor hairbrush. At least there was no vast, intimidating lobby to cross, wondering if she could make it without either stumbling over a potted palm or tripping on a rug. She had never been the most self-assured of adolescents, and sometimes she wondered if she had improved all that much since, in spite of all the very expensive schooling that seemed to make her only more self-conscious.

She drove slowly through the village, seeing places she had walked with Kiel only a few days ago, and making a rude noise at her maudlin sentimentality, she swerved into the parking lot of a supermarket, where she bought herself a bottle of grapefruit juice and a hunk of cheese, with a box of crackers that was already going stale as soon as she opened it. She hadn't even counted her money, but there was no point in being more extravagant than she had to be. At least not until she had paid her tab at the motel.

With no particular goal in mind, she drove on down toward the Ocracoke ferry landing and, on impulse, took one of the free ferrys across Hatteras Inlet to the northern end of Ocracoke Island. She had never been down that far south on the outer banks, for it was in another county and they had no listings there, but it was well worth seeing. As narrow as Hatteras Island, there were plenty of places where you could stand in the middle and practically throw a stone into both ocean and sound. Besides, she rationalized, it would be a shame to return to Florida, if worse came to worst, without ever seeing the place where Blackbeard operated; for all she knew, she might be cruising over the very spot, right now, where he and Lieutenant Maynard engaged in the fatal fray. Her history of the area was spotty at best, having been put together from bits and pieces gleaned from clients and locals over the past few months.

She rolled off the ferry and pulled over to allow the more determined of the vacationers and fishermen to streak on south to the village of Ocracoke, and when several carloads of fishermen got out to try their luck in the rain there at the inlet, she decided she'd get out too. For all the northeast wind, it wasn't cold and she could no more bear to be cooped up in her car with her thoughts than she could in her motel room. Remembering that brief moment on the beach just before she had stepped on whatever it was that had cut her foot, she wondered if she were an escapist. She had had a feeling then of being able to physically outrun her problems. Was that behind her precipitate trip south?

At least her foot seemed improved, which was a good thing, considering that she had not brought along so much as an aspirin, much less the antibiotic the doctor had prescribed. Come to think of it, she had paid for neither the pills nor the visit.

With a dawning horror, she realized who must have paid the tab, and she had taken it as her due. Lord, if he needed any reinforcement for Randy's accusations, she had certainly provided them. She was so used to having her father settle everything for her that it hadn't occurred to her that Doctor Whelan wasn't on the Silverthorne payroll.

The bandage, even with her rubber flip-flops, didn't last more than a few yards and so she stooped and unwrapped it, tossing it into a covered container near the ferry landing. Saltwater was supposed to have curative powers, so let it cure.

She waded through shallows, walked the hard, low-tide shoals, all with no notice of the dramatic seascape surrounding her. Dark gray clouds raced over water that was churned to a pale, milky green, and the audible wind lashed frostings of white spume across the surface. She trod the pink-white sand carelessly, setting herself up for another accident, had she but considered it, but for once, her luck held, and she returned to her car after a while with nothing worse than a dripping head and drenched clothes.

Reconsidering her initial idea of going all the way down to Ocracoke village, she caught the next ferry back to Hatteras. As it was, she had just about enough gas to see her home and she'd best not waste it. Too wet to go traipsing into a restaurant, she stopped by a seafood takeout place and invested in a plate of clam strips, the least-expensive thing on the menu, and surprisingly good, at that. She ate in her room, watching an inane game show on TV to keep her mind—well, if not exactly occupied, at least numb.

It was almost four by the time she reached home and already growing dark with the clouds that had followed her up from Hatteras. The wind had shifted now, bringing with it a tendency to thunder and lightning.

There was no sign of Jasper's Ferrari, nor of the Porsche either, although Kiel's garage remained enigmatically closed. Ada would still be sleeping and she hoped Jasper hadn't made a pest of himself by coming around every hour or so to wake the poor woman up.

Letting herself inside, Willy decided that Ada Willits could take care of herself in that respect. She had been doing just that for a good many years now, according to her son, who talked far more about his family than he should.

Sure enough, there was a puddle in the living room and another in the bedroom and by the time she had mopped them up, she realized that unless she wanted to top off her list of personal calamities with a streaming head cold, she'd better do something about her wet clothes. Running a tub full of steamy water, she searched out her last pair of clean jeans and a long-sleeved shirt. At least now that she was among the ranks of the unemployed, she'd have more time for such mundane chores as laundry.

The phone rang just as she was about to climb into

the claw-foot bathtub and for a minute she considered letting it ring. She hadn't the self-restraint. Naked, she padded across the living room, stopping to hook her screen door on the way, and when she reached the phone and picked up the receiver, it was to hear an expressively firm click on the other end. She lifted her shoulders disdainfully. So much for that!

The next time it rang she was heating herself a can of she-crab soup, adding a good-sized dollop of sherry for good measure. She caught the phone after the third ring this time and heard her father's impressively stern voice asking for—no, demanding—Wilhelmina.

"Hi, Jasper," she said impassively. "This is Mina."

There followed a tirade that Willy promptly tuned out, even considering at one time putting the phone down long enough to go stir her soup. Finally, Jasper came to the end of his breath, or his indignation, or both. Willy told him evenly that she had been to Hatteras overnight and that, no, she wasn't broke, nor was she starving, and the "What's this I hear about your having to see a doctor," was nothing more than a minor cut foot.

She could almost feel his letdown at that. He would have enjoyed having something drastic to hold over her, like a pregnancy, or the latter stages of malnutrition—anything to enable him to deal swiftly and peremptorily and then force her back into his suffocating care. "Look, Jasper, I don't want you to come over tonight. I'm tired and I'm having a bowl of soup and then I'm going to hit the pillow for at least the next twelve hours. Then, and only then, will I see you. Call me tomorrow . . . after ten."

So saying, she hung up the phone, halfway expecting

him to call back immediately. For that matter, he'd be more likely to barge in on her unannounced, and she got up and locked her door, turning off all the lights except the dim fluorescent in the kitchen. It was enough to see by, although it occurred to her that if Jasper could see her now, eating her soup from a plastic bowl with a stainless-steel spoon, drinking hot tea from an exquisite bone-china cup with a chipped rim that she had picked up at a yard sale, he'd have apoplexy. She had grown up with rock crystal that rang in the correct key, bone china whose renowned hallmark could almost be read through its translucency, and silver that required a full-time servant just to polish it.

After putting her few dishes in to soak, she wandered restlessly from room to small room. With the windows closed against the rain it was growing impossibly stuffy and she slid open the door to the porch, which was somewhat sheltered from the direct weather. For a long time she stood there, hearing the muffled roar of the ocean, hidden behind a dark curtain of rain, and the sound was a solid, somehow reassuring background for her own thoughts. She yawned widely and considered going to bed.

Tomorrow would come quickly enough, and with it, Jasper and his demands and recriminations. It was only a little after seven, though, and there'd be empty, wakeful hours at either this end of the night or the other, for no matter how much she loved to lie in bed and daydream in a delicious half-awake state, she could never sleep more than eight or nine hours at a stretch, and sometimes not even that.

Lately, not *nearly* that! She switched on the small radio and searched out the few stations that came through the static. She should get herself a stereo and then she could have music on tap, of just the sort she was in the mood for. She might buy a few opera albums—*The Pearlfishers,* perhaps.

But first she'd better see to getting herself a job. And before that, she had to deal with her father and send him on his way convinced that she was better off without his omnipotent assistance.

As her mind veered from one thing to another, her restlessness not helped by the increasingly close flashes of lightning, she wrapped her arms about her and stood staring blindly out at the house across the way. Cutting through the rest of her mundane problems like a hot knife through butter came the conviction that the answer to all her problems could be summed up in one word: Kiel.

With an impatient oath, she turned to the cabinet over the refrigerator and pushed aside the few bottles of wine to find her medicinal brandy. A panacea for seasickness, homesickness, shock and frostbite, plus Lord knows what else, she'd see how it was as a buffer against unwanted yearnings.

Yearnings! She hadn't *yearned* for anything since she was eleven and Jasper had told her remotely that, no, she could *not* become a veterinarian and she most certainly could not have the outstandingly pregnant mongrel bitch someone had dumped in their neighborhood as a bad joke. The dog had had a touchingly apologetic look on her face and Willy had wept while Astin summoned the local authorities.

An hour and a half later the level of brandy in the bottle had sunk by more than an inch and Willy was harmonizing badly with the music of a country-western station. "I'm tiddly," she crowed to herself, carefully replacing the jelly glass on the edge of her coffee table. She digested that information during a break in the program while the announcer read off a list of bluegrass festivals to take place in the area during the month, and then she uncurled herself and made her unsteady way to the five square feet she called her kitchen and put on a pot of coffee.

A loud blast of thunder tossed a ball of blue fire around the room, and before it subsided, she splashed water over her jeans, swore roundly and continued the makings. The electricity could go off any minute and she'd gone about as far with the brandy as she could; time to reverse the trend with black coffee before she went to bed.

The coffee was made—barely—when the lights blinked and went out and the compressor on the refrigerator groaned as if to say, not again! She located a mug and poured herself a cup of the thick, black liquid in the dark. She had hardly finished more than half of it when the pounding started. The lightning had not abated and she was tucked up on the sofa, all her doors and windows closed tightly, and her head moved slowly in the direction of the door. It was impossible to see a thing, and when between bursts of thunder she heard the pounding again and a voice yelling for her to open up, she hurried across and threw open the door.

Jasper, darn his hide, couldn't wait for morning to tear a strip off her, but even so, she couldn't leave him outside in all this.

"Jasper, I told you I didn't want to see you tonight!" she yelled over the almost constant rumble. All she could see was a tall figure shrouded in a dark raincoat.

It could have been Blackbeard himself, for all she could tell in the eerie, flickering light. "Why couldn't you have waited? I'm ready for bed and I don't need a session with you to help me sleep, darn you!"

"Well, I must admit I'm disappointed, but then, maybe I rate higher as a soporific than poor Jasper," Kiel growled sarcastically as he dropped his gleaming raincoat into a heap on the floor.

She caught at the door facing to keep her knees from buckling. "What are you doing here?"

"Under the circumstances, that's a damned stupid question," Kiel retorted, taking her arm and steering her unerringly across to the sofa. "Sit down, Willy! If I have to hog-tie you, you're going to sit there and listen to me until I'm through talking. Is that clear?"

"No, it is *not* clear!" she flared back, jerking her arm vainly against his relentless grip. "This is *my* home and you have no right to come barging in here when I've locked the door! That's breaking and ent—"

He interrupted her and his voice was not pleasant to hear. "You opened the door willingly enough, even if you did think it was Jasper." He sneered the name. "Who's Jasper, another string to your bow?"

So he didn't know. Well, be damned if she was going to straighten him out on *that* score. If he thought that of her, then she may as well be sure he didn't change his opinion. At least she'd get rid of him before she did anything irreparably stupid, like squandering the last thing she had left—her pride. "If he is, it's no concern of yours," she told him haughtily, the aftermath of the brandy strengthening her dignity.

Kiel was quiet for so long that she was strongly tempted to rush into speech just to fill the uncomfortable silence, which was probably just exactly what he was waiting for. Oh, he'd make a great lawyer; give them enough rope and all that!

Grimly, she crossed her arms and clamped down on her bottom lip. She could wait just as long as he could and then we'd see who'd be the first to crack.

Outside, the storm seemed to be abating. Here on the banks, it could rain inches in mere minutes, the weather changing with dizzying speed, thanks to the conflicting currents of the warm Gulf Stream and the cold Labrador Current, and right now she felt as if both influences were raging through her body: the brandy-induced heat making her feel uncomfortably flushed, and the chill in her heart growing more noticeable by the moment.

"Where were you?" he asked after a while. The harsh anger seemed to have left his voice and now it held only the most impersonal sort of interest.

"I went to Hatteras," she admitted grudgingly.

"Any particular reason, or just a whim?"

"A whim. Now, if you're satisfied, maybe you'll leave me to get some sleep."

"Are you certain you can sleep without a—what did you call it, a session?" Before she could register her shock and disgust, he barked out a question. "Did your going have anything to do with Melanie?"

She caught her breath as that one hit her in the solar plexus. "Why should my actions have anything to do with Melanie?" she asked, her voice tight and several notes higher than usual.

"No reason at all, except that she had a rather self-satisfied smirk on her pretty little mug when I drove her to Norfolk to see Randy this morning."

It took a minute to digest this latest news, and even then she wasn't at all sure how to take it. So Melanie was gone. Certainly she hadn't gone without a protest, not when she had already declared her intention of having Kiel as a replacement.

"No questions?" he taunted in the oppressively still darkness.

She shrugged, unseen. "Why should I have any questions? What you and Melanie choose to do has nothing at all to do with me."

"I thought you might just possibly be wondering why she was going to visit Randy Collier in the hospital, but since you aren't at all curious, I take it you've been satisfied on that score."

Cautiously, she ventured, "What score?"

"The fact that you already knew that Randy was my half-brother and Melanie's fiancé—off and on—leads me to believe you've had a cozy little chat with Melanie herself. Knowing that puss, she wouldn't pull any punches, so what I want to know is, did what she told you have anything to do with your deciding to run away?"

"I didn't run away!"

"No?" The one word was loaded.

"No! Now, if you're finished, I'd appreciate it if you'd get out of here! What you and Melanie and Randy Collier work out among the three of you is of no possible interest to me, and I don't intend to waste an evening being bored with a lot of silly soap-opera plots!"

"Whew! She must really have drawn blood with those kitten claws of hers. What did she tell you, Willy?"

She didn't want to discuss it. She didn't want to remember because, if she went into that hateful subject at all, she'd end up either howling her eyes out or taking a swing at him, damn his tough, tormenting hide!

"Well?" he prompted softly, and then, when she still refused to be drawn, he reached for her, and in the darkness she hadn't enough warning to escape until it was too late.

"There's one surefire way of getting a reaction from you, you damned little cat. You've claws of your own, enough to take care of a spittin' kitten like Melanie, and the very fact that she came out of the fray with her fur unruffled and her purr intact leads me to believe she must have dealt you a really stunning blow." He inhaled against her newly washed hair as he held her struggling body in an entirely effective grip. "What was it, Willy?" he asked softly. "What hurt you so badly you had to run away? Or shall I tell you?"

"No . . . no, I don't want to hear it!" she blurted turbulently, her voice thickening with the emotion that was beginning to destroy her self-control.

He ignored her outburst, turning her deftly in his arms, and when for an instant her own arms were freed, she began to pound on his chest with her fists. Struggling against his superior strength only seemed to excite him and the low laugh that feathered along her cheek did serious damage to her resistance. She moaned his name, but he caught it with his mouth and forced it back against her teeth, grinding a kiss into her lips that seemed to go on and on.

"By this time, I know how to handle you, Willy Silverthorne," he growled long moments later when he finally raised his head for air. His arms still held her captive, not that she would have had the strength to try and escape now—as he darned well knew, to her eternal shame!

She lay limply in his arms and one of his hands came up to stroke the hair from her damp forehead. "Getting a little steamed, aren't you, love?" he taunted, and when she would have risen indignantly, he held her in place easily by the simple device of a well-placed hand on her chest. "No you don't, not yet. We still have some pretty important ground to cover and you're not getting up from here until you hear what I have to say. Shall we make it the hard way or will you cooperate?"

Her lips thinned determinedly, not that he could see them.

"Speechless? Good," he commented. "Now, to get down to it, you know by now what I'm doing down here. That irresponsible half-brother of mine came down to get established in the area; then he was to dash home, marry his childhood sweetheart and bring her on down here to live hapily ever after. Unfortunately, he stopped writing and stopped calling, and since the Colliers, the Fredericks and the Faulkners—at least, this Faulkner—are pretty closely tied in business affairs as well as family matters, I began to get a lot of flak about it." He took time to shift her more comfortably and she weakly allowed herself to settle down against his warm, hard, clean-smelling body. "After my father died, to give you a brief background, my mother married Ed Collier, a young engineer. Randy came along a year later, and then, when Ed died a few years ago, it was natural for Randy to take over. I'd already established a firm of my own with several offices along the East Coast and we kept a loose connection, along with another firm of marine engineers owned by Melanie's father. Melanie's been in and out of the Collier household since she was a baby, and as a sort of big brother to her, I was elected to sort out this latest in a long line of hassles between the two of them."

"Oh, so it wasn't the first time Randy had given his girlfriend a spot of trouble?" Willy asked with smug satisfaction.

He ignored her. "When someone from CCE—I don't think we need to mention any names or look far for a motive—anyway, when we got a letter from someone in the office saying that Randy was making a fool of himself over some woman—"

In spite of herself, Willy broke in again. "As I understood it, the woman was making a fool of him, for what she could get out of him," she said bitterly.

A hand closed over the back of her neck and, before she could protest, began kneading muscles that she hadn't even realized were hard with tension. "It takes two," Kiel went on smoothly, his hand working its magic on her nape. "Randy's a full-grown man, and as you once mentioned, a man doesn't wear an engagement ring. There's nothing to warn a girl if he decides to play around a little."

She squirmed, feeling the heat stealing over her as the hand continued its hypnotically soothing work. "Then you don't blame the girl in question?" she ventured.

"No, nor do I blame Randy too much after meeting

164

the girl in question," he said. "Willy, my sweet girl in question." He leaned over and brushed a kiss over her eye and she shivered helplessly, torn with that dreadfully familiar longing in spite of all reason. "Is the slate clean now?"

She shifted, trying to escape the coercive hand. "I'm not sure, Kiel. You say Melanie has gone to see Randy. Does that mean they plan to get back together again?"

"Whatever they plan is their own affair. I did my bit for family and business relations, and now it's up to the two of them. I'm much more interested in recent developments in my own life."

His words brought a quivering sort of hope and she had to test it before she dared venture out of her shell again. "Aren't you afraid the girl in question might look on you simply as an even better catch? You did say—or rather, Melanie did—that she was only out for what she could get."

"I am—an even better catch, that is," he admitted with a total lack of self-consciousness, "and anyway, it's not too hard to understand a girl's being influenced by that sort of thing. By her very nature, a girl has to think of security, but don't think I'm blaming you, darling. I understand—"

He got no further. Twisting herself away from his arms, she drew herself up and away from him just as the lights blinked back on and the reluctant refrigerator groaned back into service once more. "Oh, so you understand, do you?" she blazed. "How very noble of you! All ready to forgive and forget just so you can lure the mercenary little working girl into your bed! Men! You give me a pain!" She turned away from him, her shoulders rigid as she crossed her arms over her chest in an effort to keep from swinging at him.

She was so furiously disappointed she could have howled! For a minute there she was so sure he had come to know her better, to like her as a person and to realize that if she loved a man, it wouldn't matter to her if they had to live in a tin-roofed shack on collards and croakers.

"Get out," she said in a voice that was devoid of feeling. "Just get out and leave me alone before I call the sheriff and have you put out."

"Dammit, Willy, what have I said *this* time? It seems to me you spend too damned much time analyzing every word that passes between us! When I make love to you, you understand me well enough; it's only when we get all tied up in words that you turn into some skittish little hedgehog! Now make up your mind, for God's sake, because I can't take a hell of a lot more from you!"

"Nobody asked you to take anything from me!" she charged, turning to glare at him from blazing eyes. The yellowish overhead fixture cast shadows across her cheeks from her thick, long lashes and it served only to emphasize the effects of too many sleepless nights. She looked dragged out and she knew it, and it didn't make things any easier for her, especially as she had a damned good idea that his world was running over with women who looked like Melanie.

Without another word, she turned and stalked off into her bedroom, slamming the door and dragging a chair up under the knob in case he had any ideas about carrying the fight further.

Evidently he hadn't, for she heard him slam out the

door and the house practically shook with his stormy exit, and she told herself she was glad to be finally, irrevocably finished with him. She would allow herself exactly one night to cry her stupid heart out and then, come tomorrow, she'd dry her eyes and never shed another tear over any man!

Chapter Ten

By morning Willy had convinced herself that it had all been her own fault. Whatever had happened to her usual easygoing dispositon? She had never been this way before, flying off the handle at the slightest provocation, backing herself into a corner with her quick defensiveness. Before she had time to come to her senses, she dialed Kiel's number. It rang several times and she could picture the black, utilitarian phone on his bedside table. She had been in his room only once, but it had been impressed, every feature of it, indelibly on her mind.

Could he have gone to work already? As usual, she had no idea of the time, for the alarm clock was electric and functioned according to the vagaries of the power system. The sullen sky outside gave no real clue as to the time of day, and suddenly terrified lest she awaken him, she was on the verge of hanging up when she heard the click that indicated that the receiver had been picked up. Her breath caught in her throat and she steeled herself not to slam down her own receiver with cowardly haste.

"Hello," came a muffled mumble at the other end, and she stiffened. "Hello, who is this?"

The voice was clearer now in its impatience, the feminine drawl unmistakable, and with her soul shriveling like a flower after a killing frost, she slowly replaced the receiver.

It rang almost immediately and she ignored it. Finally it stopped, and as if she were released from a spell, she moved away, her bare feet silent on the cold linoleum. So much for last night's cool, pat explanation. Melanie and Randy—Kiel might have thought he had the two of them all lined up to fit back into the same old slot, but hadn't Melanie herself said she'd decided she'd rather have Kiel than his brother? Little Melanie, for all her deceptive fragility, was a very determined lady, and regardless of what Kiel might have decided, he obviously wasn't proof against a willing female in his own bed, especially not when she looked like the magnolia-skinned Melanie.

Shaking herself out of her stunned lethargy, she began, almost by accident, to give the apartment a thorough turnout. Spilled coffee led to a smeary wipe-up, which led to a mopping, and once she got into the swing of things, she found the unusual exertion was just what she needed to work off an excess of energy.

By the time the phone rang again, bringing her back to the present, the windows were sparkling, the refrigerator defrosted, and she had tackled the cabinets, where for almost six months she had jammed and juggled things in an effort to fit everything into her skimpy kitchen space.

"Hello," she answered warily. After all, she couldn't hide forever, and if it was Kiel, she'd simply hang up, but she rather thought she'd seen the last of that gentleman. From the looks of her, Melanie could keep him occupied for the immediate future, at least.

"Mina? May we please talk now?" her father demanded with exaggerated patience.

She had forgotten all about Jasper's being here, something he would have found impossible to believe, and she promised to be ready to go out to breakfast with him in half an hour. "What time is it, Jasper?"

"It's seven-twelve. Why?"

She could almost see his perplexed irritation when she suddenly burst out laughing and hung up the phone. Seven-twelve, and it had been at least two hours ago that she had called Kiel. Good Lord, no wonder Melanie had been asleep. A little earlier and no telling what she would have blundered into.

She selected one of her few really nice day dresses, a brown linen sleeveless with white binding, and she was glad to discover that her foot had healed enough for her to wear white pumps. May as well spread it on a bit for Jasper, so he'd at least accept the fact that she hadn't gone native.

By the time she heard the low growl of her father's Ferrari, Willy was all ready and she pulled the door closed after her and ran lightly down the stairs, congratulating herself on an award-winning performance. She had even gone so far as to make up her face with more than the usual dash of lipstick, and was surprised at the difference it had made. Her father should be flattered, had he but known it.

Jasper waited for her beside his low, muscle-bound car and Willy immediately noticed the change in him. At first she thought he looked younger, for he had lost a few pounds and his health-club figure showed no hint of his excesses. Not only that, but the sunlamp tan he achieved year round, which Willy thought somehow pathetic, considering he lived in Florida, covered the slight flush that had increased with the years. The greatest change was his hair. Prematurely white, he had always taken great pride in the thick crop of hair that contrasted so dramatically with his dark skin, but now it had gone a medium shade of brown and she was suddenly aware that he looked every one of his forty-nine years, and then some. Poor Jasper . . . it seemed his very zeal to make himself appear younger had the opposite effect.

"Hello, darling," she said with more warmth than she had done in years. She embraced him easily, with none of the restraint she had expected, and it came to her that she felt a little bit sorry for him. "How've you been? You look marvelous?"

He kissed her on the forehead. As tall as she was, she had inherited that height from him and his arm fit easily across her shoulders as he turned her face up to study it. "I've been well enough, and off-hand I'd say the same applies to you—contrary to my fatherly fears. Looks as if you might have been having too good a time partying lately, but on the whole . . . I approve." He laughed and she hugged him to her side.

"I'm starved, Jasper. Where do we eat?"

"My hotel does a pretty good spread. Lord knows, I've had time enough to check it out while I cooled my heels waiting for you to turn up. When you go for independence, you don't use any half-measures, do you?" He held the door open for her and she tucked her skirt in, allowing her eyes to stray to the brown shingled cottage across the way. Was that a movement behind the screen? Impossible to say from this angle, but she hoped it was. She hoped that it was Kiel Faulkner and that he saw her being solicitously tucked in by an attractive and obviously wealthy man. Another string to her bow, he had suggested. Well, just so he didn't think *he* was her only hope! If she could maintain this fine edge of anger, she just might make it till she grew enough scar tissue so she didn't bleed to death!

For the first time in her life, Willy reacted to her father as one adult to another, and it was a heady experience. Her newfound independence raised her up to his eye level, and unexpectedly she found a touching hint of vulnerability in the man she had always held as slightly above and off to one side of humanity.

Over herring roe and blintzes they talked of Willy's experiences as a newly fledged real-estate saleswoman and Jasper related some of his own earlier exploits in the same field, to her amused enlightenment. When he suggested she might enjoy joining him on his leisurely drive up the coast to Nova Scotia, she found the courage to mention Breda for the first time. So far, as if by silent mutual consent, they had avoided the subject of Jasper's third wife.

Before Jasper could answer, there was a tap on the door and a bellboy brought a note, which Jasper read and pocketed, dismissing the boy with a bill.

"Desk says a fellow's been making inquiries about someone driving a car like mine. Do I look like a car thief to you?"

"One with exceptionally good taste, at least," she teased, dismissing the incident and returning to his suggestion.

"All right, Mina," her father interrupted, "I can see you aren't quite ready to commit yourself to a couple of weeks of my steady company, but at least let me send for your things and have you moved into my suite for a visit. That should give you more time to make up your mind."

Her first impulse was to refuse, and then she thought,

Why not? A change of scenery might give her the objectivity she needed to decide on her next step. It was a cinch she couldn't remain at the beach—or anywhere else outside her father's company—without a job; and now that the season was well under way and the place swarming with college students, most of the positions would be filled. She didn't hold out much hope of her own field, if what Matt had said about the economic scene was true.

They returned to her apartment and Willy took a slightly wicked pleasure in watching Jasper's reaction to the place she had spent over half a year in. He tried manfully to hide his distaste, but it was as if he suddenly found himself in the tourist section of a commercial liner instead of ensconced in the plush comfort of his own Lear jet.

"I won't be a minute," she promised him. "Have a seat, or you might enjoy my porch. I've a fabulous view."

Selecting the things she knew her father favored from among her skimpy wardrobe, she packed enough for two days. He might have to get used to seeing her in jeans and off-the-rack casuals if his visit lasted much longer than that, she thought with a wry smile. This just wasn't Jasper's sort of beach. In his perfectly creased sharkskins, his navy blazer with the yacht-club colors and the ascot carefully arranged at his throat, he looked somehow diminished—or was that because Willy unconsciously stacked him up beside a tall, sun-bronzed creature in jeans and worn-deck shoes?

Drat! She had promised herself to forget Kiel Faulkner and all he stood for, and even now she could still see the way the light got behind his dark eyes, making them incandescent, could still smell the particular fragrance of his healthy male flesh and feel the touch of his hands as they made their sure way over her body.

To clear away the unwanted memory, she started chattering as soon as she joined her father, and as she pulled the door to after her and locked it, she asked about Breda once more.

Jasper carefully handed her bag into the back before turning to answer her question. "Mrs. Coyner-Silverthorne is cruising in the Caribbean with friends. We were both to go and then I got a call from—Well, you know, of course, that I've pretty well kept up with your progress," he said almost shamefacedly. "At any rate, I decided to take a drive up north and drop in on you, and so my lovely wife went on alone." A bitter smile appeared for a moment and then faltered. "Not that I expect she's still waiting for me. No, darling, it looks as if I may as well relinquish my fond and foolish dreams of having a son and settle for grandsons, providing my daughter obliges me before I'm too old to teach them a thing or two."

Willy had paused with her hand on the open door and now she turned impulsively to her father and wrapped her arms around him. "Oh, Jasper, you old sweetheart, you—as if you weren't still young enough to start a dozen families!" She reached up the few inches necessary to kiss him gently. "Don't count on me to do the honors, though. I have a feeling I might be the career-woman type."

He handed her into the low-slung car as if she were infinitely precious to him, and by the time he had opened his own door with a courtly flourish and lowered himself behind the wheel, all traces of moisture had gone from her eyes.

She stayed three days at the plush beachside hotel and the two of them saw the sights, with Jasper doing his level best to assume the mien of the average tourist when it was all too obvious that he considered himself far from the average anything. On Thursday afternoon, he took her down from his third-floor suite, a bellboy following along behind with her one case, and they paused just outside the door to speak to an acquaintance of his.

While Jasper was assuring the man that they had little to worry about as far as the the first tropical depression of the season was concerned, Willy allowed her eyes to stray across the parking lot to a field of wild flowers, and then her eyes blinked and returned slowly to the parking lot where Jasper's Ferrari baked in the summer sun. It was not the Ferrari, however, that had caught and held her stunned look; it was the silver-gray Porsche that was parked beside it, one door open with a long, jeans-clad leg extending from it.

She gulped, and when Jasper turned and took her elbow, she could hardly breathe, much less speak. Walking stiffly beside him, she tried to tell herself that she had made a mistake. After all, there was more than one 928S on the roads, so why not another one here at Nags Head?

Deep inside her, where something heavy and cold lay in the pit of her stomach, she knew it was no mistake. Kiel Faulkner was out there waiting for her, and for the life of her she couldn't think why. After the way they had parted, she would have thought he'd be glad to see the last of her.

Unless—rational thought had flown out the window as she came nearer to that one long, powerfully muscled leg extended so carelessly across the cracked concrete paving—unless he was here to throw a monkey wrench in the works by telling her father about her behavior or, at least, what he thought was her behavior as far as Randy was concerned.

With a panicky reaction more in keeping with a schoolgirl, Willy turned impulsively to her father. "Jasper, maybe I will go to Nova Scotia with you, after all."

But it was too late. Looming before them was Kiel Faulkner, who looked as if he could take her neck between his fingers and snap it the way the boys at the docks headed shrimp. "Hello, Kiel," she managed with a poor excuse for a smile. "Have you—I'd like you to meet—"

"Where have you been these past three days," Kiel demanded, his eyes ignoring Jasper to bore straight through Willy.

"Here, now," broke in Jasper, who was not at all used to being dismissed.

"You keep out of this, dammit! Willy"—he turned to glare at her—"have you been here with this—this antique Casanova?"

"Now you listen here, my good man," Jasper blustered, but Kiel turned on him, forcing him to step back precipitately. "I'm not your good anything, you swine, and if I ever catch you hanging around her again, I'll take you apart, limb by limb! Come on!" He grabbed Willy by the wrist and practically threw her into the car, slamming the door after her. She managed to keep her fingers from being sliced off, and when Kiel slung himself in beside her and roared out of the parking lot, leaving a stunned Jasper standing there with her suit-case in his hand, she was still clutching her hand, totally beyond speech.

They passed the corner of Wimble Court at a speed that should have drawn every patrolman out of Manteo, and when he kept on going without even slackening, Willy stole a frightened glance at his grim profile. She had never before noticed that his jaw was made of steel, with whitleather stretched tightly over it, or that his nose cut the air before him like some slashing broadax.

"Where are we going?" she managed when he slowed down to ten miles above the legal limit.

"Shut up!"

She shut. They were headed either for Bodie Island Lighthouse or for Oregon Inlet, and when they roared past the black and white lighthouse and kept on going, she began to thaw out. The marina. The *Good Tern*, and unless he planned to drown her immediately, then he must have some good reason for what amounted to virtual kidnapping.

A thought occurred to her. All her life, she had been guarded against such an occurrence, for the only child of a man as wealthy as Jasper Silverthorne was con-stantly vulnerable. Wouldn't it be a hoot if she were being held for ransom by a man who was almost as well-to-do as her own father? Maybe they could trade . . . Randy for her. She giggled, from pure nerves.

"I'm glad you see something to laugh about in all this. Believe me, when I'm through with you, you won't be doing much laughing!"

She remained quiet, her insides quivering with a sensation that didn't bear examining, and when Kiel pulled up at the marina in a spray of marl and dragged

177

her from the car, pulling her stumblingly after him, she hurried along, her high-heeled pumps threatening to throw her with every step. Not until he more or less shoved her into the small tender did she utter an outraged protest, and that he countered with a succinct word.

As incensed as she was, there was little she could do when he ripped through the lazy-afternoon quiet with a roar of his small, powerful outboard, and by the time they reached the moored ketch, she was determined to hold her peace until she had him where she wanted him; then, and only then, would she let go with a blast that would have him thinking twice and three times before he ever dragged another woman away from her father.

The deck shifted gently under the weight of two boarders and Willy lurched awkwardly for an instant before she regained her balance. Oh, fine! Just the way to make an impression, falling flat on her face! She reached down and pulled the high-heeled shoes off and dropped them carelessly as she stood there, calculating her next move.

Kiel had gone to the stern and was making fast the small tender, ignoring her completely, and finally she could stand it no longer. "Would you care to explain your outrageous behavior, or am I to understand that you just couldn't wait for my company a minute longer?"

"If that's the case," he sneered, "then it looks as if I'm no more particular than you are, doesn't it?"

Her breasts heaving turbulently, Willy glowered at him while he did something to the lines that led to the anchor, and then it dawned on her that he was preparing to get under way.

"Just a damn minute there, Kiel Faulkner, you can't do this!"

"It looks to me as if I'm doing it, and stop swearing. I'll take your word for it that you're a tough, liberated cookie without your having to prove it every other breath."

"I—I'll have you up on white slavery charges," she threatened, and then wished she'd kept her mouth shut when she saw the look he leveled at her.

"You're asking for it, Willy, and believe me, I've never disappointed a lady yet," he said silkily.

"No, I'll just bet you haven't! You—you probably earned the *Good Housekeeping* seal of approval for outstanding performance!"

He grinned at her as he reached around the console and started the throbbing engines. "Make that the *Woman's Home Companion* and I'll go along with you."

Infuriated, she turned her back on him, staring at the creamy wake that sprang up behind them as the *Tern* headed smoothly out into the inlet. She'd just ride it out. Not another word would she say until he told her what he was doing and why.

"There's a slab of fresh tuna in the refrigerator. I'd suggest broiling it with butter and pepper and maybe a dash of lemon."

"And you can go straight to hell and take your tuna with you," she seethed.

They went under the bridge and he laughed without bothering to turn around. "Your stomach'll conquer you, Willy Silverthorne, even if I can't manage it."

With the sudden stricken feeling that he just might be right, Willy turned, to stare at his back. The wind was blowing his dark hair around his head and the sun, sinking lower and lower into the Pamlico Sound behind them, washed his broad shoulders and lean hips with copper, leaving his legs from the thighs on down dark with the shadow of the boat. Had she ever thought even for a minute that she could wipe him out of her mind? She must have been mad.

With a helplessness born of conflicting emotions, she dropped down onto the cushion-covered lockers as they followed the tortuous channel out the inlet. Once on the other side of the breakers, she felt the engines slow, and when all motion except for the slight roll ceased, Kiel strode lithely forward and she heard the hum that signaled the lowering of the forward anchor. She waited fatalistically while he lowered the stern anchor, and then, when he nodded to the hatch, she got up and followed him below.

"Fight all gone? You must be either hungry or seasick," he remarked as he opened the refrigerator and took out a slab of pink fish.

Silently she watched the preparation of the meal. If she had suspected him of deliberately cultivating a few culinary tricks to capture her interest in the beginning, she knew she was wrong. He moved too surely as he went about the business of grilling the fish, tossing a simple salad and pouring the wine on the gently rocking sailboat without spilling a drop.

From time to time as they ate, she felt his eyes on her in a speculative way and she ignored him, pretending absorption in her food, although for once she was totally uninterested in what was on her plate. The tuna was something to be pushed around with her fork as her mind raced frantically in circles, always coming out at the same place. She knew with a dreadful sort of fascination that after tonight, nothing would ever be the same.

Finally, he stood up and said, "All right, Willy. No point in punishing your plate with your fork any longer. Get in there." He nodded to the door behind her, which she knew led to his stateroom. Inside the compact, well-designed space was the V bunk and little else, and she raised stricken eyes to him.

"Kiel . . . not this way, please," she whispered, still sitting rigidly in her chair at the convertible table.

"Then what way, Willy? In your apartment? In a hotel suite? You name it, you've got it," he told her bitterly, moving toward her relentlessly so that she had to stand or be overrun. "What's the matter? You were interested enough not too long ago. Is it that fellow at the hotel?" His voice was filled with contempt and something that sounded strangely like hurt . . . which was impossible. "I'll match my material possessions against his and give you something he can't match, Willy. Ten years and a wedding band. How's that for a bargain?" He flung at her, forcing her in through the narrow door so that she stumbled and fell against the bunk.

She closed her eyes against the hard accusation she saw in his, and when she felt his hands on her hips, she turned away from him, but he pulled her back, catching her under the knees and throwing her legs up on the triangular mattress. Something inside her was crying and she had no idea the sounds were escaping until she felt the cool wetness on her face.

There were sounds from behind her and she heard the rasp of a zipper and then he was beside her, turning her over so that he could open her dress down the back.

She was beyond physical resistance, but she whispered, "Please, Kiel, not when you hate me so much."

The laugh that tore from him was not a pleasant thing to hear. "Hate you! God, how I wish I could! Can you imagine what it's like to despise someone and love them at the same time so that you end up hating yourself for your own weakness? That's what you've done to me, Willy Silverthorne." Her dress had been pulled aside roughly and now he lifted her and tugged it from under her and threw it aside. "I came down here prepared to show you up for what you were and prove to Melanie once and for all that she had nothing to worry about. You can imagine how I felt when I fell under the spell of your own particular brand of sex appeal within days! I told myself a man could afford to like his work and still do a good job, but when I lost all perspective and began doubting the things I knew were true about you, then I should have had the sense to get the hell out and let Melanie sort out her own problems."

His hands had commenced that hypnotic stroking now, and as she felt his touch on her throat and down her shoulders to her breasts, Willy knew she had to say something before matters went any further.

"Kiel . . . about Jasper. You don't understand," she began hesitantly.

"Oh, I understand, all right. A man like that, thinking he's over the hill and then getting the come-on from a girl young enough to be his daughter—"

"But that's just it, Kiel! I *am* his daughter! Jasper's my father!"

The hand stopped. It was as if all life ceased for a moment of suspended animation, and then the breath was ripped from his lungs as if she had struck him in the middle. "Oh, God, Willy, don't play these games with me. Please, girl." His voice was a hoarse parody of his usual assured tones and Willy turned and caught him up in her arms. "Please," he groaned, "you've got me where you want me—that is, if you *do* want me. I'll marry you, I'll do anything you want—only, Willy, from now on I'm the only man in your life. I'll take care of any needs and wants you have, regardless of what they are, is that understood?"

She buried her face in his throat and once more the tears forced their way out from under her lids from a heart that was unbearably full. "Oh, Kiel, as if I could ever even look at another man, as if I had ever really had a chance after that first time you showed up with a measuring cup in your hand." She laughed shakily. Her hands were stroking his back and he insinuated himself closer so that she was aware for the first time that he had on as little as she did.

His mouth captured hers and all the pent-up emotion was there for her to read and answer, and as her lips parted under his own, he began to tell her in a hundred ways that did not require words how much he needed her. She was busy answering him with her lips, her hands and her whole body, and outside there was only the sound of the waves caressing the hull of the *Tern* and an occasional creak as the boat moved with the currents.

After a while, he drew slightly apart from her overheated body, laughing unsteadily from deep in his chest. He caught her hands and held them both in his and he whispered, "Behave yourself, you wanton creature. Who taught you these things?"

With a self-satisfied little purr, she answered him. "You did. I couldn't sleep nights for thinking what I wanted to do to you and what I wanted you to do to me, and so now all I need is a willing partner to practice on and I'll be as good at making love as I am at selling real estate."

He rolled her over and applied a hand smartly to her bottom. "Don't go searching one out, girl, or you'll land in more trouble than you can wade out of. I think you'd better tell me more about this Jasper character for a starter."

She did, and his reaction was all she could have wanted. After the first moment when she almost thought she heard a tremor in his voice, Kiel told her all the thoughts that had gone through his mind when he saw her drive off with the attractive man in the racy-looking sports car. "I knew then that regardless of what you did, you were going to have to settle for me or I wouldn't be responsible for my actions. I reasoned that a girl who had been around some would be ready and willing to settle down if a man offered her a wedding ring and I was willing to take a chance on holding you."

"Oh, darling, except for a silly farce where I ended up with my pride hurt, I've never been even faintly interested in any man other than as someone to go out to dinner with."

"Oh, I can guarantee you three meals a day and as many snacks as you think you can handle."

"Kiel, you know all about my past limitations, my lack of experience where men are concerned—" Willy began hesitantly.

"A lack which I intend to rectify immediately, if not sooner," he put in.

She caught her breath, determined to get through with what she had to say, and then go on from there.

"Kiel, what I mean is—well, Melanie. I called, you know, that morning after—"

He hooted. "Was that you? Honey, what you must have been thinking!" Leaning over to brush the tumbled hair from her face, he smiled warmly into her eyes. "Precious, Randy and Melanie came back and stayed at my house until they could leave for Atlanta. I slept on the porch and didn't ask any questions about what went on inside, but I can tell you right now, that miss wasn't any too happy to be waked up before daybreak."

"It wasn't before daybreak," she protested. "At least, not much before."

Settling her head in the crook of his shoulder, Kiel went on to tell her something that made her heart grow almost too large to be contained. "Sweetheart, there hasn't been a woman in my bed since the day I met you, a fact that hasn't done much to improve my disposition, but if you want to keep me sweet and happy, then you know how to go about it, because from now on you're the only woman in the world who can do the job."

"Oh, Kiel, you do know, don't you, that you're the first man ever to open the box my heart came in? I was scared to death you were going to keep the wrappings and throw away the gift," she gurgled into the firm flesh of his throat.

"I'll have to admit that the wrappings were what first caught my fancy, woman. And incidentally, what about this father of yours? How's he going to take having a full-grown son sprung on him, especially after I trailed him up and down the beach by that car of his and then did my damnedest to find out who he was . . . not to mention kidnapping his only child in broad daylight."

She laughed aloud. "Oh, he'll adore it! He's something of an old pirate himself, and just the other day he was telling me he had all but given up trying for a son and was ready to settle for a grandson."

Growling low under his breath, Kiel suggested that they see if they couldn't manage to present him with his heart's desire about nine months hence, and that brought on a reaction that left them both trembling breathlessly. "Oh, God, I love you, Willy Silverthorne —Willy Faulkner. I'll promise to feed you in the manner to which you've become accustomed, and sooner or later you'll learn to get as big a thrill from wind and water as you do from handling a fast car, but your biggest pleasure will be—"

She laid a finger over his mouth. "My biggest pleasure will always be you, darling. I've been saving my appetite for a dozen lifetimes for you, and from now on I plan to feast!"

Silhouette ❦ *Romance*

15-Day Free Trial Offer
6 Silhouette Romances

6 Silhouette Romances, free for 15 days! We'll send you 6 new Silhouette Romances to keep for 15 days, absolutely free! If you decide not to keep them, send them back to us. You pay nothing.

Free Home Delivery. But if you enjoy them as much as we think you will, keep them by paying the invoice enclosed with your free trial shipment. We'll pay all shipping and handling charges. You get the convenience of Home Delivery and we pay the postage and handling charge each month.

Don't miss a copy. The Silhouette Book Club is the way to make sure you'll be able to receive every new romance we publish before they're sold out. There is no minimum number of books to buy and you can cancel at any time.

This offer expires September 30, 1982

Silhouette Book Club, Dept. SBN 17B
120 Brighton Road, Clifton, NJ 07012

Please send me 6 Silhouette Romances to keep for 15 days, absolutely free. I understand I am not obligated to join the Silhouette Book Club unless I decide to keep them.

NAME _____

ADDRESS _____

CITY _____ STATE _____ ZIP _____

IT'S YOUR OWN SPECIAL TIME

Contemporary romances for today's women.
Each month, six very special love stories will be yours
from SILHOUETTE. Look for them wherever books are sold
or order now from the coupon below.

$1.50 each

Hampson	☐ 1 ☐ 4 ☐ 16 ☐ 27 ☐ 28 ☐ 40 ☐ 52 ☐ 64 ☐ 94	Browning	☐ 12 ☐ 38 ☐ 53 ☐ 73 ☐ 93
Stanford	☐ 6 ☐ 25 ☐ 35 ☐ 46 ☐ 58 ☐ 88	Michaels	☐ 15 ☐ 32 ☐ 61 ☐ 87
		John	☐ 17 ☐ 34 ☐ 57 ☐ 85
Hastings	☐ 13 ☐ 26 ☐ 44 ☐ 67	Beckman	☐ 8 ☐ 37 ☐ 54 ☐ 72 ☐ 96
Vitek	☐ 33 ☐ 47 ☐ 66 ☐ 84		

$1.50 each

☐ 5 Goforth	☐ 29 Wildman	☐ 56 Trent	☐ 79 Halldorson
☐ 7 Lewis	☐ 30 Dixon	☐ 59 Vernon	☐ 80 Stephens
☐ 9 Wilson	☐ 31 Halldorson	☐ 60 Hill	☐ 81 Roberts
☐ 10 Caine	☐ 36 McKay	☐ 62 Hallston	☐ 82 Dailey
☐ 11 Vernon	☐ 39 Sinclair	☐ 63 Brent	☐ 83 Hallston
☐ 14 Oliver	☐ 41 Owen	☐ 69 St. George	☐ 86 Adams
☐ 19 Thornton	☐ 42 Powers	☐ 70 Afton Bonds	☐ 89 James
☐ 20 Fulford	☐ 43 Robb	☐ 71 Ripy	☐ 90 Major
☐ 21 Richards	☐ 45 Carroll	☐ 74 Trent	☐ 92 McKay
☐ 22 Stephens	☐ 48 Wildman	☐ 75 Carroll	☐ 95 Wisdom
☐ 23 Edwards	☐ 49 Wisdom	☐ 76 Hardy	☐ 97 Clay
☐ 24 Healy	☐ 50 Scott	☐ 77 Cork	☐ 98 St. George
	☐ 55 Ladame	☐ 78 Oliver	☐ 99 Camp

$1.75 each

☐ 100 Stanford	☐ 105 Eden	☐ 110 Trent	☐ 115 John
☐ 101 Hardy	☐ 106 Dailey	☐ 111 South	☐ 116 Lindley
☐ 102 Hastings	☐ 107 Bright	☐ 112 Stanford	☐ 117 Scott
☐ 103 Cork	☐ 108 Hampson	☐ 113 Browning	☐ 118 Dailey
☐ 104 Vitek	☐ 109 Vernon	☐ 114 Michaels	☐ 119 Hampson

Silhouette Romance

Coming next month from
Silhouette Romances

Reluctant Deceiver by Dorothy Cork

When Merlyn flew to Hong Kong under false pretenses, her plan backfired. Sullivan, the only man she would ever love, refused to believe in her innocence.

The Kissing Time by Jean Saunders

When Julie is hired as Vince's research assistant, she learns that when the gorse is in bloom on the Scottish tundra, it is indeed, "the kissing time."

A Touch Of Fire by Ann Major

When Helen Freeman books a room in a Paris hotel she finds that a handsome stranger has prior claim to it and he intends to take full advantage of their impromptu introduction.

A Kiss And A Promise by Anne Hampson

After Judith broke her engagement with Alexis she thought their love had died. But when she went to live in his house as a nanny to his young nephew, she discovered that love can be rekindled.

Undercover Girl by Carole Halston

Reporter Kelly Lindsay was thrilled at the prospect of living undercover in Palm Beach. But she had never imagined that she would fall in love with the subject of her exposé!

Wildcatter's Woman by Janet Dailey

After years of divorce, Veronica realized that Race was the same irresponsible wildcatter she'd walked out on—but he also hadn't lost his heart-stoppingly powerful, sensual magnetism.

**Look for *Daring Encounter* by Patti Beckman
Available in June.**

READERS' COMMENTS ON SILHOUETTE ROMANCES:

"I would like to congratulate you on the most wonderful books I've had the pleasure of reading. They are a tremendous joy to those of us who have yet to meet the man of our dreams. From reading your books I quite truly believe that he will some-day appear before me like a prince!"

—L.L.*, Hollandale, MS

"Your books are great, wholesome fiction, always with an upbeat, happy ending. Thank you."

—M.D., Massena, NY

"My boyfriend always teases me about Silhouette Books. He asks me, how's my love life and natu-rally I say terrific, but I tell him that there is always room for a little more romance from Sil-houette."

—F.N., Ontario, Canada

"I would like to sincerely express my gratitude to you and your staff for bringing the pleasure of your publications to my attention. Your books are well written, mature and very contemporary."

—D.D., Staten Island, NY

*names available on request